A Note to Readers

Although the Allertons and Hendrickses are fictional characters, many other people in this book really lived. Salmon Chase was a well-known attorney who eventually served on Abraham Lincoln's cabinet. Levi and Catharine Coffin were Quakers who helped run the Underground Railroad.

It may seem unusual that Fred Allerton began working full-time at his father's factory when he was only eleven. In truth, this was quite common in the 1840s. Child labor laws didn't exist until fifty years later, and many boys only went to school until they were ten or eleven years old. Designing ways to let steam power increase production in the factory wasn't unusual, either. Mechanization of factories during this time period was common, and often teenaged boys and young men led the way.

When the Hendrickses left for California in 1849, they became part of a huge movement of people to the West Coast. Hundreds of thousands of people traveled the Oregon Trail to California and the Oregon Territory. Men, women, and children walked most of the two thousand miles over prairies and pumice fields, mountains and rivers, in hopes of building a better life.

ENEMY
or
FRIEND?

Norma Jean Lutz

BARBOUR
PUBLISHING, INC.
Uhrichsville, Ohio

To Richard Lodato, whose determination is much like
Fred Allertons!

© MCMXCVII by Barbour Publishing, Inc.

ISBN 1-57748-258-1

Published by Barbour Publishing, Inc., P.O. Box 719, Uhrichsville, Ohio 44683
http://www.barbourbooks.com

Member of the
Evangelical Christian
Publishers Association

Printed in the United States of America.

Cover illustration by Matthew Archambault.
Inside illustrations by Adam Wallenta.

CHAPTER 1

Fred's Steam Engine

"More coal in this one, Sammy Joe," Fred Allerton called out over the chugging sounds of the steam-driven engine.

"Yes, sir. I see it." The young black man, his face shiny with sweat, opened the door of the brick firebox. His huge muscles bulged as he rammed the wide silver shovel into the nearby mountain of coal. One time after another, he filled the shovel full and threw the load into the blazing firebox.

The mammoth steam engine nearly filled the basement of the Allerton Furniture Factory, and Fred knew every bolt, valve, and piston. He watched Sammy Joe for a moment, then moved around the engine to check the gauges. It was just as he thought. The idea of using two fireboxes rather than one was creating the exact results he'd expected.

He'd worked nearly every night the past week to install the improvements. Now he and Sammy Joe were able to sustain a more even amount of steam-driven power, which turned the whirring woodworking lathes upstairs. One firebox tended to keep the boilers either overheated or underheated. It was not only dangerous, but a waste of coal as well.

Sammy Joe slammed the iron door of the firebox shut with the shovel, making it clang. He turned to Fred and gave him a big grin. "It's doing its job just fine now, ain't it? Just like you said it would."

Fred picked up two oilcans and handed one to Sammy Joe. "Other men tested the idea before me. All I did was read the manuals and learn from their mistakes."

Together they nursed the moving parts with plenty of oil to keep it running smooth as silk.

"Your papa, he wasn't too sure."

Fred smiled. "Papa's not liked the engine since I first installed it a year ago."

At age fifteen, Fred had been working at the factory for nearly four years; but the early years were spent sweeping floors and carrying water, followed by hours in the accounting offices. Then he was promoted to sanding, polishing, and varnishing the fine pieces of furniture. Papa said he would trust Fred with the steam engine only after he'd proven himself in every other area of the factory.

Sammy Joe jerked his thumb at the giant flywheel. "Mr. Allerton says this thing makes him nervous."

Fred laughed. "Nervous is all he'll admit to."

"But the machine sure does turn out a heap of bedposts in a big hurry."

"And chair spindles and chair legs and plenty of other pieces. But Papa still doesn't like all the noise and smoke."

Sammy Joe nodded his head. "Your papa's a quiet man. Likes quiet things."

"My laboratory's quiet, but he doesn't like it too well, either." Fred waved toward the room at the far end of the basement near the stairs. There Papa had allowed him a small space for his experiments. His books on science and electricity lined the shelves as well.

Sammy Joe chuckled. "He be worried it won't *stay* quiet."

"I haven't blown anything up yet."

Sammy Joe's deep-chested laugh sounded out again. "Yet!" he teased.

Fred and Sammy Joe worked well together. It had been Fred's idea for Papa to hire a black person in the factory. Papa was dead set against it. He wasn't convinced that black men could learn as well as white men. But Fred had insisted. He'd looked all around Cincinnati to find just the right person. And he found Sammy Joe working hard sweeping streets for the city. Fred liked him immediately. Sammy Joe's city supervisor described him as reliable and hard working, and the Allertons had found that description to be very accurate.

By the time Fred and Sammy Joe had oiled the moving parts and checked the valves a few times, it was time to fire up the second box. As they moved to that side, the day's delivery of coal came tumbling down the coal chute, causing a cloud of black dust to rise in the air. It was at that moment that Papa came down the stairs. He waved his hand in front of his face to clear the air.

"I can remember a day when all I had to worry about around here was sawdust," he said with a grimace. "Now there's coal dust, smoke, soot, and too much noise."

"Good morning, Papa," Fred called out. "Installing two fireboxes was exactly what was needed. Come and look."

"Morning, Mr. Allerton," Sammy Joe said. "Fred's got her singing right nice." He opened the door of the second firebox and proceeded to shovel in the coal.

"You'll be pleased to learn we're using less coal now, too," Fred told his father. "More power, less fuel. That's good, don't you think?"

Papa only nodded. Ben Allerton always appeared tense and nervous when he came into his son's domain. Fred had tried everything he knew to put his papa at ease. He'd explained in detail about the safety plugs made of lead alloy. If the water level fell and uncovered the metal piece—which was near the fire—the plug would melt, allowing steam to safely blow out into the fire.

The previous year, when the boiler was under construction, Fred had even taken Papa with him to the foundry. He pointed out how the boiler plates were made safe with standardized rivet holes that matched and held firm. No leaks.

More recently, however, Fred had finally accepted the fact that his father was hopelessly old fashioned and would probably never get used to the mechanized age. Now his papa stepped cautiously about the basement to look at the gauges and listen to Fred explain about the changes. He nodded as Fred talked.

Presently he said, "I'm relieved to know it's doing what you wanted it to. It certainly cost enough for the renovations."

Fred smiled inwardly. He'd worked on the accounting books long enough to know that Papa's margin of profit would allow him to rebuild the entire factory and still be in the black. But Papa had always been frugal with his pennies. And Mama was exactly the same way. Unlike some women who wasted their husband's earnings on silly pretties, Emma Schiller Allerton didn't waste a thing.

As Papa moved back toward the stairs to leave, Fred said, "I'll walk up with you. Time to check the gears and belts up there." He turned to Sammy Joe. "You've got the hang of it now. Just keep filling them at alternate times."

"Just like clockwork."

"And watch the gauges."

"Yes, sir. I'll be watching."

At the stairway, Papa stopped and wrinkled his nose. "What's that I smell? Is something burning?"

Fred chuckled. "I'm surprised you didn't smell it when you first came down."

"I was fighting coal dust, remember?"

"It's from one of my experiments I was performing early this morning. What you smell is sulfuric acid."

Papa shook his head one more time. "I wonder if you'll blow us up or burn us up."

"I plan to do neither one."

The men who worked at the steam-powered lathes answered to Papa, but they also respected Fred and marveled at his knowledge of the engine that ran the lathes at which they spent long hours each day.

Alroy MacLandish, a ruddy-faced, red-bearded Irishman, was especially partial to Fred and trusted him completely. Zeb Benton worked alongside Alroy. Four lathes ran off the steam engine that Fred operated. There were two, sometimes three men to a lathe. This day as Fred came up the stairs into the work area, the men were hard at it. The sight of those lathes spinning and humming never failed to stir Fred's heart.

"Top o' the mornin' to you, laddie," Alroy called out over the noise of his lathe. "I dunno how you've done it, but my machine's not taken the least of a breath since she fired up."

9

Fred pointed to his temple. "All in the brain, Alroy. All in the brain."

Alroy gave a hearty laugh. "God be praised if we all would be given such a brain. Though it might prove a mite dangerous for some of us."

"Yeah," Zeb quipped. "If Alroy had half that much brain, he'd be dangerous."

"Watch it, Zeb." Alroy doubled up a large fist. "I'll give you an Irish hug—right around your skinny throat."

Laughter from the men echoed through the large room. Fred moved among them, joining in the laughter as he inspected each belt and all the moving parts to ensure that everything was in tip-top condition. Nothing escaped his watchful eye. Any belt that showed the least bit of wear was quickly replaced. Fred knew of factories that were constantly shutting down due to mechanical failure, but his machines were never down.

The factory's offices were located on the fourth floor. Papa's office and all the accounting cubicles were up there. The second and third floors were given over to all the hand-crafted pieces, of which Ben Allerton was so proud. The first floor and basement housed the mechanized operations.

Even though Fred appreciated the handmade furniture, with its exquisite inlays and fancy scrollwork, he also believed the pieces made by steam-operated lathes were just as nice, especially when Papa's workers put on the finishing touches.

At noon, Fred sounded the whistle that he'd installed to indicate the midday break. The break was only thirty minutes, but it gave him time to disappear into his laboratory and work. The materials he'd been using that morning were still strewn across the worktable in his laboratory. There he had lengths of insulated wire that he'd coiled about a magnet. According to the book he'd just read, this should increase the magnetism. And just as the book said it would, the magnet pulled in bigger and bigger chunks of metal.

As he worked, Fred failed to notice the jar at his elbow containing a piece of phosphorous that had been submerged in water. Turning quickly, he accidentally knocked the jar to the floor. He jumped back as the exposed phosphorus suddenly burst into flame.

"Sammy Joe!" he called out. "Bring the water bucket! Quick!"

Chapter 2

Abolitionist Meeting

Sammy Joe came on a dead run with the bucket in his hand. But the phosphorus was stubborn. He dumped the entire bucket of water on it, and still the phosphorus smoked and smoldered.

Coughing and sputtering, Fred pulled his woolen peacoat from off a nearby hook and flung it over the smoldering chunk. When he picked up his coat, the fire was finally out—but there was a hole in his coat.

Just then Papa appeared at the door. Fred looked up to see that Papa was smoldering almost as much as the phosphorus. "I told you those chemicals were dangerous," he said firmly. "They'll be in my factory no longer. Have them all out of here by tomorrow morning."

"Yes, sir," Fred replied. "But it was just an accident."

"Accidents I don't need. Tend to your work and leave the chemicals alone. Or else!"

"Yes, sir."

"Now clean up this mess. The whistle should have blown five minutes ago."

The last words made Fred feel worse than having caused the little fire. He prided himself on keeping the whistle right on time. When Papa was gone again, Fred said, "Blow the whistle, Sammy Joe. Then bring the mop." Looking at his peacoat, he added, "Mama's gonna kill me."

As the shrill whistle shrieked its order for the men to return to work, Fred could hear the lathes begin to turn once again. Together he and Sammy Joe mopped up the water and inspected the damage. The floor had a hole in it, but it was nothing the two of them couldn't fix.

"Your papa's plenty mad now. What're you gonna do?"

"First I've got to get back to the engines. Gather me a couple of crates, and at quitting time, I'll pack up the bottles. I won't be able to take them home until morning. I'm headed to an abolitionist meeting tonight."

Sammy Joe's eyes grew wide. "You gonna be at another meeting with Mr. Chase?"

"That I am," Fred said, his pride swelling a bit. "And Papa doesn't like that one bit, either."

Golden light from several hanging oil lamps shone brightly, casting shadows on the serious faces about the room. A solitary heating stove, its stovepipe directed into the fireplace chimney, erased the February chill from the simple parlor. The meeting at the home of Salmon Chase had lasted longer than any of the men had planned. Though Fred was thankful to have been included, he fought to keep his heavy eyelids from drooping.

He shifted about, trying to find a comfortable position in the fanback Windsor chair, which was feeling quite hard. He had to remind himself how long it had taken him to get to this place and what a privilege it was to be there. For years he'd begged his older cousin Timothy to allow him to attend the abolitionist meetings, but Tim would say, "These meetings are not for children. When you turn fifteen, maybe then you'll be responsible enough to take part."

That didn't make much sense to Fred, since he'd been working for Papa since he was twelve. That seemed pretty responsible, but it hadn't changed Tim's mind. Fred's fifteenth birthday had arrived a few weeks ago, and this was the second meeting he'd been able to attend.

James Birney, editor of Cincinnati's abolitionist newspaper, the *Philanthropist*, straightened a stack of newspapers and pamphlets that were spread out on a small table beside his chair. The meeting had opened with a discussion of the progress of the abolitionist movement nationwide. Then the conversation had turned to Salmon Chase's involvement in the Free-Soil Party Convention back in Buffalo, New York, the previous summer.

Salmon Chase, sitting right in front of Fred, had served as the party's leader. Fred was fully aware that the way the country's politics leaned had much to do with whether or not slavery would spread all the way out to California. That was what these men intended to prevent.

Just then, Salmon looked up as his wife, Sara, came into the room, carrying a tray holding pots of coffee and tea. In a cheery voice, she said, "If you men are going to talk until late, you'd best keep drinking up the coffee."

"Thank you, my dear," Mr. Chase said to her. "Please don't bother yourself with serving. Just leave the tray."

She smiled and nodded, setting the tray on the table beside her husband. Her wide taffeta skirts, spread over ample hoops, made a soft swishing sound as she moved. Her hair was caught at the nape of her neck and gathered into a red net snood—red that matched the brightly colored plaid dress.

Fred's sister Meg, who loved bright colors, would very much like that dress. At age seventeen, and with an attentive beau courting her, his sister was much into fashion of late. Sara quietly left the room, closing the door softly behind her.

The men poured cups of coffee, and Fred passed his mug to Tim. He, too, needed a stimulant for the late hour. As Tim handed the mug back, Fred glanced up and noticed a silver pitcher sitting on the mantel. Writing was etched on the side. The gleam from the soft lamplight made it difficult to read, but he could make out a few words. The larger letters read: "To Salmon P. Chase from the Colored People of Cincinnati." The smaller words were obscured.

Fred had heard stories from Tim about how selflessly Attorney Chase had represented runaway slaves and other black folk who could not testify on their own behalf.

Fred's eyes met Tim's at that moment, and his handsome cousin smiled and gave a little nod. Tim's nod told Fred that this was indeed the silver pitcher that Tim had told him about—the one presented to Salmon Chase from the black community in appreciation of his public service on their behalf.

Fred glanced at the pitcher again and made out the date—February 12, 1845—exactly four years ago to the month. The gleaming silver pitcher was an awesome sight in Fred's eyes. He could scarcely believe he was actually sitting in a room with these courageous, dedicated men.

The clean-shaven, balding Chase leaned back in his chair after serving the coffee and tea. "The platform resolutions we wrote for the Free-Soil Party were well thought out," he said in a clear, strong voice. "But when the opponent is a beloved war general like Zachary Taylor, it's not an easy campaign to win. The Mexican War made a hero of Taylor, in spite of the fact that he had no real political standing."

Fred knew that was true. He and Tim talked often about the Free-Soil Party's choice of former president Martin Van Buren as their candidate. In the election, the man had not carried a single state. How would the nation ever stop slavery if slavery was allowed in all the new territories?

"We've been over these issues numerous times," said Thomas Spooner, Chase's close neighbor and supporter. "You did the best you could, Salmon. Time to put this behind us and look forward."

Fred wanted to chime in his agreement to that statement, but he'd received strict orders from Tim to keep quiet. "Until you're established and gain a few years," Tim had said firmly, "you have nothing to say. Remember that."

Keeping quiet was one of Fred's most difficult assignments. Even Papa chided him about learning to bridle his tongue.

At length the conversation wound down and the men rose to go. Sara stood by the door, handing out the heavy winter cloaks and top hats to the men. Fred was a little ashamed of his woolen peacoat and cap. They seemed so childish in this setting, especially now that his peacoat had a burn in it.

As Fred firmed his cap on his head, Salmon Chase clapped a firm hand on his shoulder. "And tell me, what's the younger Allerton doing for the cause these days?"

Fred swallowed hard. "Delivering pamphlets mostly," he said, wishing it could be more.

Tim spoke up. "Fred works at his father's factory during the day and attends night school three evenings a week. So his time is limited."

The attorney gave a warm smile. "No gesture is too small in this effort. When many people donate just a little time and effort, it means we'll soon break the back of the slavocracy in this country. Keep up the good work, son."

Fred warmed beneath the compliment. "Thank you, sir. I plan to."

The Chase home was in an older neighborhood in Cincinnati, where large stately homes stood in a solemn row like strong sentinels along the street. Fred followed Tim and the others out the front door, down the wide steps, into the cold, still night. Days-old, soot-stained snow crunched beneath their feet.

While the other men climbed into their waiting buggies, Tim and Fred turned to walk down Fifth to Plum Street. At age thirty-five, Tim was still unmarried and lived in two small rooms above a millinery shop on Seventh. Fred envied his cousin's independence and privacy. If he lived alone, he could experiment to his heart's content.

As they fell into step, Tim said, "The meeting went well, don't you think?"

Fred couldn't imagine a meeting of abolitionists not going well. "Very well," he answered.

"We're expecting a delivery of new pamphlets to arrive this week. Will you be able to distribute—perhaps on Saturday?"

Organizers back East had urged all abolition workers to distribute pamphlets to public places such as stage stations, eating establishments, and the open markets.

"I'll find the time," Fred told his cousin. "You can count on me."

"I knew I could."

They quickly covered the blocks from Fifth up to Seventh, their footsteps on the frozen snow echoing off the tall buildings that lined the street.

"Tell me, Fred," Tim asked, "is your papa still trying to stay neutral on the slavery issues?"

Fred gave a shrug. "We don't talk about it much."

"But he doesn't forbid you to attend these meetings. That says something."

Fred gave a slight smile. "I guess he knows I'd sneak off if he forbade me. I'm determined to follow my conscience in the matter."

"Uncle Ben changed his mind and allowed you to install the steam engines in the factory. Perhaps he'll change his mind about this as well."

"Perhaps." Papa had allowed the steam engines, but Fred knew that Papa did not and would not ever trust the machines.

"How's the steam engine doing?" Tim asked, tugging at his cloak to pull it closer about his shoulders. "Turning out bedposts and chair spindles by the dozens, I take it?"

"Exactly that. Since the engine was installed, I've helped Papa more than double the factory's output."

"Double? He surely must be impressed."

"High production doesn't impress Papa," Fred reminded him. "You know that. He still believes the boilers will blow any minute."

"Can't George Lankford put his mind at ease? After all, George installed some of the first engines on the Lankford steamboats years ago."

"George helped me a great deal when I first began, and he still comes in to inspect things once in awhile, but Papa's mind is made up."

Tim shook his head. "It's good to be stalwart about the right things, but Uncle Ben's thinking seems to stem more from fear than from resolution."

Fred thought about that for a moment. "I'm not sure about the fear. It's just that Papa clings to sameness. I've never known him to take many risks."

Tim chuckled. "That's Uncle Ben all right. And what of your laboratory? You haven't blown that up yet, have you?"

Fred laughed. "As a matter of fact, I had a little fire just today. Nothing serious. But Papa says all the chemicals must be out by tomorrow."

"And what will you do with them? Your mama surely won't allow them in the house."

"I plan to build a shed in the backyard. I believe that'll be the best solution."

"Your own little place. That does sound like a capital idea." As they approached the door that led to Tim's stairway, Tim nodded his head toward it. "Want to come up for coffee? I can make a strong pot over the spirit lamp. I may even have a cracker or two lying around."

"Mama will be waiting up for me. I best get on home."

"When Dot agrees to marry me," Tim said, "I'll have homemade cakes and punch to offer you. Then you won't be able to refuse." Fred wasn't too sure. Though he thought the dark-eyed Dorothy Ludlum was quite lovely, he liked his cousin much better as a bachelor. "I'll stop by Saturday to pick up the bundle," Fred said, "just as soon as I can get away from the factory."

"It's agreed. Good night. Take care now on your way

home." Tim tipped his black silk top hat, then stepped inside the doorway and closed the door behind him.

Fred picked up his step as he hurried home, anxious to get in out of the cold February air. Their home was located north of the city in an area just west of the German community. It was a good distance to walk, but Fred was used to it. Mama would probably have a loaf of *Hefeküchen* waiting for him.

He shoved his gloved hands deeper into the pockets of his peacoat and thought about the evening. It made him feel almost like a grown man to be able to meet with the group. In a few years, he'd be doing even more for the abolitionist cause. Ever since he was a small boy, he'd felt strongly about the wrongfulness of slavery. It bothered him that almost all the furniture shipped from the Allerton Furniture Factory found its way down the Mississippi and into the fashionable homes of wealthy slave owners.

As he approached his house on Everett Street, Fred saw the welcome glow of lights in the windows of their sturdy two-story home. Dormant trailing rose vines twisted in naked coils around the arch at the front iron gate. He lifted the latch, let himself in, and went around to the back door. He could almost smell the *Hefeküchen,* and his mouth was watering.

Perhaps he could hide his peacoat and ask Meg to patch it secretly.

CHAPTER 3

The Hendrickses' News

Mama and Meg were busy in the kitchen when Fred entered. The aromas of good food filled the place. Keeping his back to the door, he slipped out of his coat and folded it neatly.

As he started to walk across the room to Meg, Mama said, "Papa says the coat will need mending from the burning." She spoke without turning from the stove. Meg shot her brother a smile from across the room.

So the family had been told of his latest escapade. "It's just a little hole," he said. "It won't take a very large patch."

"A perfectly good coat," Mama said. "Now a patch it will have." She shook her head.

Fred went to her and kissed her cheek, stepping over the fat cat named Goldie, who tried to push against his legs. He knew how Mama hated to waste anything. "Your patches are so neat and fine, I won't mind a bit wearing a patched coat," he told her. He winked at Meg and hung his hat and muffler on the pegs by the door.

"Where your smooth talk comes from," Mama said with a sigh, "I cannot tell. No one I know in the family has it." She turned to him now as though to study his face.

"Ah, but you never met Papa's papa," Fred said with a flourish. "Being the successful Boston shipping merchant that he was, I'm sure he was silver-tongued." Though Papa talked very little about his boyhood years before his parents died, Fred did at least know that much.

"Wash up and put this food in your smooth-tongued mouth," Mama said sternly, setting a plate of beef and vegetables with spaetzle noodles on the table. "We know too little about your Opa Allerton to say."

Just then Fred heard Julia come bounding down the stairs and through the hall. "Look, Fred," she said, running to his side. "Look at my arm!" Her arm was bound up in a small splint from the wrist to the elbow, covered with a white bandage. She wore it like a badge of honor.

"Julia," Mama said firmly, "young ladies do not run."

"What happened to you?" Fred handed his coat to Meg, who held it up to study the hole.

"Skating!" she replied. "On the canal."

"With the boys," Meg put in.

"Playing crack the whip can be dangerous," Julia said, her eyes sparkling. "And fun!"

"I guess the same can be said for smelly chemicals, eh Fred?" Meg fetched Mama's mending basket from the corner of the kitchen. "Mind if I be the one to patch the coat? My stitches are as neat as Mama's."

"I don't mind," Fred answered.

Mama rolled her eyes heavenward. "A lady, my Julia is not yet. Cracking a whip—with boys, no less. Ach."

Fred sat down to eat. He was ravenously hungry. As he lifted his fork to dig in, Mama touched his arm. "Cannot a word of thanks be returned for this food?"

Guiltily, Fred bowed his head and gave thanks, then shoveled in big mouthfuls. "Did it hurt?" he asked Julia between bites.

"Something terrible. It still hurts some. But," she added, "Edwin Bradley helped me up off the ice and apologized for cracking the whip so hard." With a giggle, she said, "It was almost worth it."

"It cannot be my daughter that speaks like this," Mama remarked, wiping her hands on her apron.

Julia's remark about Edwin Bradley took Fred by surprise. But then he looked at his younger sister's sparkling blue eyes and wide smile. Julia didn't just talk—she bubbled and gushed like a mountain stream. Perhaps, Fred mused, she *was* attracting boys to her side. How different she was from quiet, doe-eyed Meg.

"What were you saying about our grandpapa Allerton when I came in?" Julia asked.

"Mama wonders where Fred got his smooth tongue," Meg explained as she found a piece of wool to match Fred's peacoat. Goldie jumped up into her lap, and she put the cat down on the floor again. "Fred thinks perhaps it came from Grandfather Allerton."

"I wish we'd known Grandfather and Grandmother Allerton." Julia started to pull out a chair, when a noise at

23

the door caught her attention. "There's Papa. We'll just ask him." She ran to the door.

"I don't think Papa will be in much of a mood to discuss anything about me tonight," Fred said in a low voice to Meg.

Meg just smiled. Fred used to despise his mild-mannered older sister. Now he was ashamed of the way he used to torment her. Being friends with Meg had proven to be a great asset in his life.

"Papa," Julia said opening the door. "What was your papa like? Mama wants to know. Was he a smooth talker?"

Papa looked around the room at his family. His eyes fell on Fred, and Fred knew immediately that his papa was still angry. "You can take my cloak, Julia," he said.

Julia took the heavy cloak and hung it on the peg. Fred knew that Papa had been home for supper earlier, then had gone back to the factory to work until late. He'd done that almost as long as Fred could remember.

"The coffee is hot," Mama said, and Papa nodded. "You want it in the front room?" Mama asked.

"The kitchen is fine," he answered.

"Papa, you didn't answer me," Julia persisted in her usual way. "Does Fred talk like your papa?"

Papa was sullen. "That was a long time ago, Julia. I was only nine when he and my mama died." With that he went to the basin to wash, then stepped out to the back porch to throw the water out.

"He'll probably tell us when he gets over being upset about you and that silly fire." Julia plopped down in the chair beside Fred. "Did you go to the meeting with Cousin Timothy tonight?"

Fred nodded as he scooped up the last bites of his supper.

"Was Mr. Chase there?"

"That he was," Fred said proudly.

"My teacher says all abolitionists are selfish rabble-rousers who want to destroy the economy of the entire nation," Julia said. Turning to Mama, she asked, "May I have another piece of *Hefeküchen*? I'm still hungry."

"Fetch it yourself," Mama told her. "Your two legs are working."

"Your teacher is wrong," Fred said firmly. "If she took the time and effort to meet and talk to people like Salmon Chase and Levi Coffin, she'd know right quick that she is wrong."

Papa had returned and sat down at the table to drink his coffee. Julia jumped up and cut more of the sweet bread, placing it on a platter and setting it on the table. Meg paused from her patching and helped herself to another slice.

"It's not good to tell your sister that her teacher is wrong," Papa said solemnly.

"I don't know why I can't say she is wrong when she *is* wrong," Fred said curtly.

"Fred," Mama scolded, "such a tone to speak to your papa."

"It's a matter of record that violence follows the abolitionists wherever they are," Papa said, pulling out the newspaper from his coat pocket.

"It's a matter of record that abolitionists stand up for what is good and right and fair," Fred countered. "And that rouses others who care nothing for the rights of the black man to violence."

"And what about the rights of the states? Are we to govern every person's life and tell them how to live and how to conduct business? That makes government too strong and powerful."

"Our government was designed for freedom for every man. Why should a man be excluded because of color?"

"Benjamin, Fred," Mama interrupted. "Please. Peace in our home is needed."

Fred stood to his feet and grabbed the outdoor lantern from the hook by the back door. Papa's blindness frustrated him to no end. "I'd like to build a laboratory shed in the backyard," he said as he lit the lantern. "I'm going to look to see where I might start it."

"Here's your coat," Meg said, standing to hand it to him. "All finished."

"Thank you," he said. "Papa? May I have permission to build a laboratory out here?"

Papa was quiet a moment. "Better there than in my factory," he said without looking up.

Fred went out, closing the door with more force than he had intended. How could Papa be so impossible?

Holding the lantern high, he stepped off paces along the back fence between the henhouse and Mama's garden. There'd be just enough room. The night was bitter cold, and in his anger he'd forgotten to grab his hat. He pictured the structure's size. It could be built out of scrap lumber from the factory. Perhaps he could even purchase a window to put in it. Later, he might install a small iron stove. He could make one himself from scrap iron he found at the railroad yard. A noise at the gate made him whirl about. "Who's there?" he demanded.

"Just me," came a deep voice. Tall, lanky Stephen Hendricks appeared from the shadows into the lantern light. "Evening there, Fred. Do you always take a lantern to the privy with you?"

Fred laughed and strode over to shake his friend's hand.

"Fine joke, my friend. I didn't even hear you ride up." He turned and pointed toward the wooden fence. "I'm going to build a laboratory out here. I was just stepping off the dimensions."

"Your papa finally kick you out of the factory?" Stephen said with a wide grin. At eighteen, the long-legged boy was lean as a rail and full of mischief. Stephen and his family had been friends of the Allertons ever since Fred could remember.

"Just the chemicals," Fred told him. "We had a little fire today."

"What's a 'little' fire? Sounds pretty frightening to me."

Fred chuckled. "Papa sure thought so. But Sammy Joe and I had it out in a minute. Phosphorus bursts into flame unless it's covered with water. I accidently knocked it off a shelf."

"I wouldn't know phosphorus from a hole in the ground," Stephen told him.

"It doesn't matter. You don't need to. What brings you over here so late?"

"Papa sent me over to tell you folks our news."

"Your news? That sounds mysterious. News about what?"

"Papa and I've been talking about it for days. We just this evening came to a decision. We're selling the mercantile, packing up, and heading for California."

Fred nearly dropped the lantern.

CHAPTER 4

Damon's Decision

"Stephen, this can't be true," Fred argued. "Why? Your family's so successful here. You're so. . .so settled."

Fred was thankful for the dim light. His eyes were growing hot with tears. Lucy and John Hendricks were like a second set of parents to him. And Susannah and Stephen were like his brother and sister. He couldn't imagine life without them.

"You know how we keep reading news about the discovery of gold," Stephen said. "Hundreds of people are heading for California."

"Your papa's not going to pan for gold?" Fred had never heard of anything so crazy. Uncle John wasn't like that.

But Stephen shook his head. "Not a chance. But think of all those people, Fred. Papa says the first merchants in the area will be the most successful ones. We aim to have the first and best mercantile in Sacramento City.

Fred thought about that for a moment. "Of course. That does sound like good planning." He lowered the lantern slowly, letting the impact of this news sink in. John Hendricks, unlike Fred's papa, had always been a man of adventure and a lover of excitement. "I guess you better come in and tell the others," Fred told Stephen.

Stephen stepped closer now. "Fred, don't tell Meg yet, but Damon Pollard is going with us."

"Damon? But he can't! What about Meg? He can't just leave her." Fred knew his sister would be devastated if her beau left Cincinnati. The young artist had been seriously courting Meg for a year or more, and wedding plans were expected any moment.

"He believes he can do better in California than here. But let's allow him to tell her and not us."

Fred only nodded, but already he was planning to give that Damon Pollard a good talking to. Somehow, some way, *he'd* make Damon come to his senses.

Fred handed the lantern to Stephen. "Take this while I grab an armload of wood." Gathering as many logs as he could carry, Fred allowed Stephen to go before him across the porch to open the back door. "Ahoy everyone," Fred called out. "Company's here."

"Stephen," Mama said with a smile. "A nice surprise this is. But so late."

"Sorry to disturb you so late, Aunt Emma," Stephen said,

going to her and kissing her cheek. "But Papa said I should ride over to tell you folks our news."

Fred took the wood to the wood box and put a log on the fire in the fireplace and two pieces of kindling in Mama's cookstove.

After Papa, Meg, and Julia had come back to the kitchen from the front room, and after Stephen was duly served a thick slice of *Hefeküchen* and a mug of coffee, he excitedly told them of the Hendrickses' plans to go west.

Fred's family was as shocked as Fred, their faces growing serious. All except Julia, that is. "What fun!" she exclaimed. "A new exciting place. I should like to travel to California one day."

"Julia," Mama scolded, "shush." She shook her head. "Such a long, long way. So much Lucy must leave behind."

Stephen nodded, reaching down to pet Goldie, who was entwining herself around his legs. "We've talked about that. But Papa and Mama feel that the temporary sacrifice will be worth it in the end." Turning to his uncle Ben, he added, "Papa wants to talk to you about the possibility of storing some of our furniture at your factory. Until we're ready to send for it, that is."

Papa nodded. "Of course. There's plenty of room. We'll *make* room."

Fred knew that Papa and John Hendricks had not always seen eye to eye on many issues—especially that of the abolitionist movement—but they'd been close friends since childhood.

Meg leaned forward, resting her folded hands on the table. "When are you leaving?" she asked Stephen.

Fred studied her worried face. Had she already guessed that Damon was going as well? Damon worked right alongside John and Stephen in the mercantile and had practically been adopted by the Hendrickses following his uncle's death. Perhaps she surmised he wouldn't stay behind.

"Papa plans to sell the mercantile as soon as possible. We'll be burning the midnight oil for a few days as we take full inventory. We want to be in St. Louis as soon as possible. We've been told the wagon trains like to start in early spring, which would get us into California by fall."

"Susannah traveling in a covered wagon," Meg said almost to herself. "I can hardly imagine such a thing."

Fred knew she was thinking about the dangers they'd face. The trip across the mountains and deserts was grueling and riddled with unspeakable hardships.

"We're all mighty excited about the possibilities," Stephen said. "Papa's received a letter from an old friend named Abbott Goddard. He's already out there, and he says that the time is ripe." He drained his mug of black coffee and stood to go. "That's what clinched our decision."

Fred had to admit that it did sound a little exciting.

"Thank you, Aunt Emma," Stephen said politely. As Papa stood, Stephen reached over to shake his hand. The lean Stephen stood a few inches taller than Papa. Stephen always stood straight with his shoulders back and his head erect. "Papa and Mama send their best, and they expect to see you all at our house on Saturday night."

Papa moved to the door. "Fred and I will see you out."

Fred jumped up and grabbed the lantern that Stephen had set on the sideboard when they came in. The three walked around the side of the house to the front street, where Stephen's horse was hitched.

"Is Damon Pollard going with you?" Papa asked after Stephen had swung up into the saddle.

So Papa had caught on.

"Yes, sir," Stephen answered. "He is."

Papa nodded. Fred knew he was concerned for Meg. Damon had more than proved himself to Papa. He was a likeable young man. In addition to being an extremely talented artist, he was also a hard worker. That had won Papa over.

Papa was quiet a moment. "We'll be very sorry to see him leave."

"Yes, sir," Stephen said. "I'll let him talk to you himself. Good night." With that, he rode off down the street back to his house just a few blocks away.

As Fred walked back inside with Papa, it was as though the anger of earlier in the day had been forgotten. Though Fred grieved that his friends were leaving, he couldn't help but be a little thankful for the distraction.

"Well, Son," Papa said as they fell into step, "looks like we may be losing Meg to a future Californian."

Fred noted a tone of wistfulness in Papa's voice.

Before going to bed that night, Fred went to Julia's room and knocked at the door. Meg was still downstairs. At Julia's answer, he opened the door and asked, "Want to get up early and go to the factory with me in the morning?"

Julia's face brightened. His younger sister loved any adventure. She especially loved the landing with all the steamboats coming and going. She never turned down an opportunity to go. "You need my help?" she asked.

Fred nodded. His quick-witted sister had already guessed what was going on.

"You're bringing the bottles of chemicals back home?" she asked.

"Two crates full. The boxes have rope handles. We can carry one between us, and I can manage the other one under my arm. Think you can do that with a broken arm?"

"Will anything explode?" The look in her eyes made Fred wonder if she hoped it would.

"Nothing will explode. Or even fizzle."

"Do I get to see the hole you burned in the floor?" She chuckled. "I wish I could have seen that."

"You'll see the hole all right. You'll have to be up before dawn. We'll have to get the things back here in time for me to get back to work and for you to get off to school."

"I can get up as early as you can. Just knock on my door."

Julia was as good as her word the next morning. Trouble was, she had to wake Meg to braid her hair because of her broken arm.

The air was still and sharply cold as Julia and Fred walked together down John Street, which headed south from their neighborhood, through downtown, all the way to the Ohio River.

In the dim morning light, as they came down the hill toward the landing, Fred could see dozens of steamboats docked. There'd been only four full weeks, in December and January, when the river had been frozen over. A mild winter meant the boats could come and go freely, which was always a blessing to the merchants of this busy port city.

Already, the landing was astir with workers loading merchandise and boats making ready to get underway for their journeys to destinations beyond. One day soon, the Hendrickses would be boarding a steamboat to carry them away. Fred still couldn't grasp the reality of that fact.

Julia paused a moment, studying the scene before them. She was probably thinking the same thing.

No one had arrived at the factory as yet. As Fred unlocked the door and let Julia in, he said, "We'll have to step on it if I'm going to get back here and blow the starting whistle on time."

"Let Sammy Joe do it," Julia said.

"Papa expects me to do it."

Julia gave an understanding nod. "That figures."

Fred lit a lantern and led the way down the darkened stairway into his corner cubbyhole.

Julia laughed right out loud when she saw the hole burned in the floor. "What did that experiment teach you?" she asked, still laughing.

"That phosphorus really does burst into flame, just like my science book told me it would," Fred replied. "I also learned to keep it out of the way of my clumsy elbow."

"Good lesson," Julia quipped.

"You take the lantern," Fred instructed. "I'll carry the crates to the top of the stairs, then we'll go."

Sammy Joe had done a fine job of packing the bottles in soft sawdust. He'd even firmly hammered on the lids.

After putting out the lantern and locking the door, Fred hoisted one crate under his arm, and together they grabbed the rope handles of the other.

"The hill will be the hardest part. We'll set it down anytime you want to rest," he told Julia.

"I can go as long as you can," she told him.

Fred didn't doubt it one bit.

As they made their way up the steep hill from the landing, the sleepy steamboats began to come to life, and their distinctive melodic whistles floated out across the cold morning air.

"A steamboat whistle is the most beautiful and yet the

saddest sound in the whole world," Julia said, panting a little from their climb.

Lost in his own thoughts, Fred didn't answer.

"I'm sure it will be that way for Meg after Damon leaves," Julia added.

Now Fred looked over at her. "And what makes you think Damon's leaving?"

"Silly boy. We all know it. It's just that no one's saying anything."

Fred was amazed. How could Julia be so perceptive? He certainly wouldn't have guessed it if Stephen hadn't told him. He never thought Damon would leave Meg's side.

"You mean Meg knows?"

"She was up late, sitting at her desk drawing sketches of him. She knows."

Meg's drawings and art were all over the Allerton home. But none were of Damon. Those she kept hidden away in the trunk in her room.

The rope was beginning to cut into Fred's hand in spite of his glove, so he knew it must be hurting Julia's hand as well. She said nothing. Oma Schiller often said that Julia had "pluck." Fred had to admit she certainly had something.

"We'll rest a minute," he said as they reached Ninth Street, which was about halfway home. Setting down the heavy crate, he added, "I'm going to talk Damon into staying behind."

"Do you think he'll listen?"

"He's *got* to listen," Fred replied. His older sister was so tenderhearted that he couldn't stand the thought of her heart being broken.

"While you try in vain to get Damon to stay, I'll be busy praying for Meg."

Fred blanched at Julia's tartness and grabbed up the crate before he was fully rested. He'd show her.

That evening, Fred had a class at Cincinnati College. It was one of his favorites—chemistry. From the beginning of the winter semester, the professor had recognized a willing student in Fred and had shown him special favor. After the first few weeks, he'd made Fred an assistant in the lab.

As he stepped from the building after class into the cold night air, Fred decided he'd stop by the mercantile, knowing the Hendrickses would still be there working. Sure enough, the store was lit up by all the gaslights in the place. The front door was shuttered with the shade drawn. He knocked, but no one came. They were probably in the back storeroom working.

Stepping into the shadows, he made his way down the alley toward the back door. As he did, he nearly ran smack into Damon. "Well, well, Fred. Bless my soul, it's good to see you." He clapped a gentle hand on Fred's shoulder. "I was just being sent home by my boss. Over my protests, of course. Lucy and Susannah went home hours ago, then brought us supper. Come on, I'll take you inside. You want to see John? Stephen?"

"Actually, Damon, I stopped by to see you."

"Me? What a fine gesture that is. Want to go inside, where it's warm?"

"Let's walk. Your boarding house is on my way home."

"Is Meg all right?" Damon asked.

Fred turned back toward the street, and Damon came along beside him. "I guess you're the only one who can answer that. That is, if you really care."

"Those are strange words coming from one who's seen my intents for the past several years."

"What are your intentions with my sister?"

"Fred, I dare say you speak as though you're the father, not the brother."

Fred turned to him as they paused beneath a gas lamp pole. "I thought I knew your intentions. Now I understand you're going to pick up and leave the city and desert her."

"Desert her? Those are strong words."

"What do you call it? If you leave, she'll be heartbroken."

"Your sister is much stronger than you give her credit for, Frederick. I have no doubt she'll wait for me. Forever, if need be."

"Why should she have to wait? Why must you go at all?"

Damon shook his head. "There's nothing for me here now. When Uncle Jack was still alive, he garnered much good support for the institute. I was safe beneath his wing as I studied to my heart's content. But the institute has never had the same support from the citizens since Uncle Jack's death. He had such a way with people. He could stir them to respond to the art world."

"You're changing the subject."

"Ah, yes, so I am. I apologize. The point is, at this time, I have nothing to offer your sister. The Hendrickses have been kind and gracious to me. I owe them a great deal. I want to help them as much as I can. Once we're established in California, I'll send for Meg. Who knows? Perhaps there'll even be opportunities for my art out there. Don't you see, Frederick? I must go and find out."

Fred wanted to be angry at Damon for hurting Meg. But Damon was about the most likeable person Fred had ever met. How could he be angry at him? Everyone who stepped foot in Hendricks' Mercantile was attracted to the dark-haired, dark-eyed young man. He was the pet of every aged widow and the delight of every child. There was something about him—a magnetism that Fred couldn't explain. It was no wonder his sister loved him.

"I wish you didn't have to go," Fred said lamely. Where had his strong arguments gone to? "I wish none of you were going."

There came those silly, childish hot tears again. He stepped away from the lamp into the darkness.

He felt Damon's hand on his shoulder again. "I've had to say good-bye many times, Fred. I've never learned to like it, but I've learned it's possible to go on with life after the good-byes are over."

Forcing his voice to be steady, Fred said, "I just think you're being mean, hateful, and selfish to go off that way. And that's all there is to it." And with that he broke into a run and ran most of the way home.

CHAPTER 5

Saying Good-bye

The following Saturday night, they gathered at the Hendrickses' home. Damon was there as well. He had called on Meg the night after he and Fred talked. Mama and Papa allowed the couple to talk alone in the parlor—something they'd never allowed previously. That meant things had taken on a truly serious nature.

Now as Susannah opened the front door to let them in, Fred's stomach knotted and churned. Many of the pictures had been taken down from the walls. A number of the smaller, more decorative items had already been packed away. Two tall wooden crates stood in the middle of the hallway. The guests had to ease around the crates to get to the parlor.

Fred couldn't bring himself to look at Damon. How could he be angry at these people whom he cared about so deeply? And yet it wouldn't go away.

As they had done on hundreds of nights before, they gathered in the parlor. Aunt Lucy was showing Mama a new recipe. Uncle John riffled through his newest abolition materials. The only difference was that Damon and Meg sat off in the corner, talking softly. And, of course, this was probably the last time they would ever gather like this. Fred couldn't understand how everyone could be so unaffected. He felt like ramming his fist through a wall.

They talked of California becoming a state—whether it would be a slave state or free—and how Zachary Taylor would fare as president. Later, Uncle John spread out maps of the Oregon Trail and explained the progress of their journey.

"We'll take a steamboat to St. Louis," he said. "There we'll purchase our wagon and oxen. Abbott says the prices for such things are better in St. Louis than farther on. There are scalpers and scavengers at the jumping-off points." The paper rustled in his hand as he pointed to the places on the map. "Abbott says we can load the team and wagon on a steamboat and ride all the way to Independence. From then on, no more boat rides."

As the conversation buzzed about him, Fred said little or nothing. Presently, Uncle John turned to him and said, "Fred, you're awful quiet tonight. Cat got your tongue?"

Fred looked at this smiling man who, in spite of a few gray hairs, was as handsome as many men half his age. Ever since he could remember, Fred had admired his uncle John. How could the man just up and leave like this?

"A lot of help you'll be to the abolitionist movement now—stuck clear out in California," Fred said. He could hear the sharpness in his own voice, but he didn't care.

"Well," Uncle John said slowly, "I believe I'm leaving the work in able hands."

"Mr. Chase says all hands are needed."

Softly, Susannah put in, "But if we're actively helping to make California a free state, isn't that helping the movement?"

Fred didn't answer.

Aunt Lucy thanked Papa for allowing them to store their furniture at his factory. "I don't want to take one more thing on that wagon than is absolutely necessary," she said. "In Abbott's letter, he said the worst problem on the trail was overloaded wagons. By storing our things, that means we don't have to give them up, but we can still travel light."

"Will you need help with the packing?" Julia piped up. "Fred and I can lend a hand."

"We can all help," Meg offered. She and Damon had moved their chairs closer to the circle around the stove, but they still sat very close to one another.

Aunt Lucy smiled as she looked around at the furniture in her tastefully decorated parlor. "I know we'll need all the help we can get. Thank you for offering."

Fred wasn't sure. How could he come and help as his friends prepared to leave him? Part of him wished he could go along. And yet he knew he couldn't leave his steam engine behind. He watched as Uncle John pulled an envelope from his pocket, producing their steamboat tickets on the *Ida Mae,* leaving in less than a week.

Turning to Susannah, Fred said, "You've never cooked over an open fire in your life. How do you expect to all of a sudden live such a rugged outdoor existence?"

The lovely, impeccably dressed Susannah only smiled. "I'm willing to learn. That's all that matters. There are others who've done it, so why can't I?" Her eyes were fairly shining with excitement.

Each of them seemed so excited, and that made Fred feel even more angry.

Before they left to go home, Papa offered up prayers for the Hendrickses. Prayers for their safety and protection, and for wisdom and sound judgment along the way. Papa even closed the prayer by asking God to heal the saddened hearts "of those of us left behind."

Fred wondered if God could really do that.

Like a gray canvas, the skies hung low over the Ohio River the day the Hendrickses boarded the *Ida Mae*. Meg's eyes had been red-rimmed for more than a week. Meg's weeping in the late night hours had awakened Julia several nights in a row, Fred's younger sister had confided to him.

The Allertons threaded their way through the bustling crowds, down the long row of steamboats, to where the *Ida Mae* was docked. Fred caught sight of the Hendrickses surrounded by friends and family. Because of their successful business, they were known and respected by scores of people in the community.

The Hendrickses were all laughing and telling funny stories and jokes as they watched their trunks being loaded. "We've asked for an extra yoke of oxen for our wagon just for Susannah's trunk of dresses," Fred heard Stephen say.

"And a wagon with an iron floor, of course," Uncle John added, laughing.

The Hendrickses had infused Fred's family with live sparks of fun and humor. Now they were leaving. How dull Fred's days would be without them.

He'd purposely avoided speaking to Damon. Even during the time when all the furniture was moved out of the house,

Fred had kept his distance. But now as they stood by the gangplank, Damon came straight toward him, capturing him with those dark eyes so full of gentleness and kindness.

"Frederick, thank you for being such a good friend." He stretched out his hand. "One day your brilliant mind will take you to incredible heights. Never give up working on your inventions. Never be afraid to follow your dreams."

Fred blinked hard, returning the handshake. "I won't, Damon. I won't give up."

"Please don't be angry at me for leaving Meg behind. If I thought it right, I would marry her in a moment of time and take her with me. But that would only be selfish. Do you understand?"

Fred wiped his wet cheek with his coat sleeve. "I think so."

Then Uncle John stepped up and gave Fred a giant bear hug. "Keep up the work with Tim and Salmon Chase. Those whom you help may be unable to thank you, but God keeps the record books."

Then it was Stephen giving an unashamed hug—then Lucy and Susannah. By now, no one cared anymore that tears were flowing. Not even Papa.

The deep, rich sound of the steam whistle and the calls for all-aboard told them that the time for parting had arrived. Lucy and Susannah waved their white-gloved hands as they scurried up the gangplank. Damon started up behind them, then came running back down to Meg, gathered her in his arms, and kissed her full on the lips in front of practically the whole town.

"I love you, Margaret Allerton," he announced so everyone could hear. Then he ran up just as the men were preparing to lift the gangplank.

The big paddles began to churn up the water, and slowly,

like an eternity, the giant white boat moved out from its spot on the landing, making its way to midriver, then came around to point west. The wide, rolling river became an open highway to carry away from him the dearest people Fred had ever known.

The Allerton house was subdued for the next several days. No one spoke much. Saturday night without the Hendrickses seemed awkward and empty. Church without them was the same way.

Fred immediately began building his laboratory, driving pilings deep into the soft ground in the backyard to support a wooden foundation. The work served to keep him distracted. His bottles of chemicals were still in the wooden crates in a corner of his upstairs bedroom. He was anxious to get the walls up and shelves installed so he could return to work.

He left his electrical supplies in his room at the factory. He continued to perfect stronger magnets and, by following the diagram in his science book, was successful in building a battery. Sammy Joe had been complaining about the rats that had invaded their basement area. So one evening, Fred connected his battery with wires attached to two steel plates. He placed the contraption along the wall where the rats had been seen running.

The next morning, to the delight of both Fred and Sammy Joe, a big old rat was lying next to the steel plates, deader than a mackerel.

"You've done it, all right," Sammy Joe said. "You smacked that nasty old rat with your electric contraption. You're a smart one, Fred, that you are."

Fred picked up the rat by its tail and laughed. It felt so

invigorating to laugh again after the sadness that had invaded his life. "Maybe I've invented an effective rat killer," he said as he went to throw the dead rodent out the door.

As he left work that evening, he made a detour over to the Cincinnati, Hamilton, and Dayton railroad station. In the railroad yards, he could always find cast-off wire, metal, and other scraps. While there, he watched as one of the newer locomotives—with C H & D in fancy golden letters scrolled on the side of the black cab—chugged into the station. The gleaming cowcatcher thrust out before the majestic cab, which was topped with a massive smokestack. The newly designed headlamp allowed this locomotive to make night journeys. The sight of the iron monster charged Fred with unspeakable excitement.

As he gazed at the machine, he wondered if perhaps he should learn more about the railroad. Everyone agreed it was the coming thing in transportation. People in Cincinnati had even talked about a railroad bridge spanning the Ohio River over into Kentucky.

Such talk made the steamboat men furious. "How can our tall smokestacks fit under any bridge?" they cried out. But Fred knew that they were crying out in fear—fear that the train would someday replace the steamboats. And Fred could easily see how it could happen. A train could go anywhere. Even all the way to California!

One afternoon, just over a week after the Hendrickses had left, Papa came down to the basement where Fred and Sammy Joe were busy working. Fred was studying the gauge after Sammy Joe had loaded the firebox with coal. The pressure was steady, just as it should be. The flywheel was spinning easily. Fred had just oiled the arms connected to the driving pistons when he looked up to see his father.

Papa didn't come down to the basement too often. Fred knew he liked to stay far from the noisy machines. "Fred," he said as he approached the area where the large engine was housed, "when you can get away for a few minutes, I'd like you to come up to the office."

Fred was puzzled. What had he done now? "Yes, sir. I can come up shortly."

Papa nodded and turned to leave.

When Papa was out of earshot, Fred said to Sammy Joe, "What could he want that would require me to go to his office?"

Sammy Joe just shrugged. "I dunno, but I saw a stranger drive up in a buggy when I was upstairs awhile ago."

Fred took the oilcan and put it in its proper place along with his other tools. "Customers come and go all the time, but it has nothing to do with me."

"Best you just get on up there and see for yourself."

"I guess you're right."

Fred went up the flights of stairs to the fourth floor and strode through the accounting room, nodding at the accountants—all of whom he knew from the days when he trained there. A more dull and boring time he could not remember. The head accountant, a studious man by the name of Jesse, looked up from his stacks of papers to give a word of greeting.

At the other end of the accounting room, Fred knocked at the door of his father's office. At his father's bidding, he opened the door and went in. Papa was sitting at his large, work-strewn desk. In a chair by Papa's desk was a man who sat with his hat in his hand. The hat was being turned around by hands that seemed to be nervous and uncertain.

Papa stood to his feet. "Come in, Frederick. I want you

to meet Edgar Purlee. Edgar, this is my son, Frederick."

The man's round beefy face was half covered by a frowzy graying beard. His small eyes seemed not to fit in the round face and reminded Fred of a pig's eyes. Hesitantly, Fred stepped forward to shake the man's hand and said a polite "Good day, Mr. Purlee." The handshake was as weak as the soft-framed man appeared to be.

"Pleased to make your acquaintance, Frederick," the man said, upon which Papa motioned them both to take a seat. He sat down again as well.

Why Papa wanted him to meet this strange man was more than Fred could figure out.

"Mr. Purlee has come to Cincinnati from Pittsburgh, Fred. Pittsburgh. The city with a great deal more mechanization than Cincinnati ever thought about."

Fred looked at Papa. What did he care about mechanization in Pittsburgh?

"Mr. Purlee worked in a factory back in Pittsburgh, Fred. He was in charge of several steam-driven engines there. He's come to me highly recommended by his former employers." Papa paused and cleared his throat. "I've hired Mr. Purlee to become my superintendent over all the mechanized portions of our business."

Papa's words hit Fred full force, like getting a stomach blow in a rough fistfight. The kind that knocks you to the ground and makes you wonder if air will ever come into your lungs again.

Fred felt himself weave on his chair.

"He'll take charge over all the men working on the steam-driven lathes, as well as the machines. In this way, that portion of the operations with be under one authority. I've been planning to do this for quite some time, but I never found the right man for the job until now. The men need someone to answer to, and I haven't time to oversee them and the men on the second and third floors both. From now on," Papa continued, "you and Sammy Joe will answer to Mr. Purlee."

"But Papa. . . ," Fred started to protest. Papa wouldn't let him finish.

"I know it'll take some getting used to, but in time you'll see this is best. Some weeks I'd like you to help upstairs. At other times, I may have you working again in accounting. It's important that you know all parts of the operations, not just one part."

Fred couldn't understand why Mr. Purlee had to be over him and his steam engine—the steam engine that *he* designed and built himself. He certainly needed no one to supervise him when he built it. Why now?

But Papa was finished discussing the issue. "You will give your new superintendent the same respect and obedience that you would give me," he said to Fred. "I believe this arrangement will vastly improve our operations."

So what was wrong with the operations at the present time? Fred wondered. But he kept silent. He couldn't bring himself to look at the round-faced, pig-eyed man. "When will this. . ." Words caught in his throat. "When will this new arrangement begin?"

"Tomorrow morning," Papa answered.

As Fred left the office and returned to his beloved machine, he felt as though he'd been stabbed in the back by the person closest to him. He felt totally betrayed.

CHAPTER 6
Edgar Purlee

A couple evenings later, Fred was working on his laboratory in the backyard. The small building was nearing completion. Julia had come out to shut the henhouse door. When she was finished, she strolled over to watch Fred work. As he struggled to lift a board into place, she stepped over and quietly held it in position so that he could hammer in the nails.

As he moved to the other side, he asked, "Bring the lantern, would you please?"

The March evening was cool, but pleasant. Julia lifted the lantern, and brought it around with her, holding it up so he could inspect his work.

Looking at the space left in the side, she said, "You're gonna put in a window."

He nodded.

"Where will you get a window?"

"George Lankford has one I can have. His men at the boatworks sometimes go downriver and salvage wrecked boats. They have bits and pieces of most everything. Even windows."

"Want me to go with you to help bring it home?"

Fred could hear the hopefulness in her voice. He knew she loved to tag along with him wherever he went. But he shook his head. "I'll just pick it up after work." He lifted another board, and fitting it snugly against the one below, he hammered it into place. Then he stood back to inspect his work.

"You've surely been quiet the past few days," Julia said. "Is something wrong? What with Meg weeping and moping about and you tight-lipped as a clam, things are about as lively as a graveyard around here."

Fred had talked to no one about Papa hiring Mr. Purlee. First of all, he was ashamed that Papa no longer trusted him. But also, there was really no one to tell. Yesterday the realization hit him that if Stephen had still been here, he would have talked it over with him—or with Uncle John. The ache Fred felt over the loss of his friends only deepened.

"Did you and Papa have another disagreement? Papa's almost as sullen as you are."

Fred looked over at his sister. "He certainly has no reason to be sullen. He has what he wants."

"And just what is that?"

"A superintendent to watch over me at the factory."

Julia gasped and stepped back as though reeling. "Are you telling me the truth, Fred? Papa did that to you?"

Her reaction pleased him. He needed someone to feel sorry for him.

"And you should see the man."

"Mean looking?" she asked, leading him on.

Fred pounded another board. "Not at all. He's all soft and fleshy—his handshake feels like a dead fish."

Julia shook her head. "I'm sure sorry, Fred. I never thought Papa would put a man over you."

"Not only will he be over me, but over Sammy Joe as well. And some days I might not be working with the steam engine at all."

"No wonder you haven't been talking. I understand now." She was quiet a minute, holding the lantern higher so he'd have better light. "Do you wish Stephen were here?"

He nodded and put a couple nails in his mouth. He was afraid if he answered, his voice might break.

"I'm sorry it happened, Fred, but it can't last long. Papa will soon see that no one can take your place. No one will care for that steam engine like you do." Julia reached up with her free hand to secure the board he'd lifted up. "I'm sure the Lord will work it all out for good. I'm just sure of it! In fact, I'll start praying about it this very night."

Fred was somewhat ashamed that it hadn't even occurred to him to pray about the matter. It certainly didn't seem like an issue that needed prayer. He just needed Papa to come to his senses. That would solve everything.

"And don't forget," Julia added as they prepared to go back into the house. "You always have Cousin Timothy to talk to."

One evening Fred attempted to approach Papa in private to discuss the situation—to explain that he needed no one to supervise his work with his own engine.

Papa, in his usual quiet way, said, "Fred, you're still a young fledgling. I've known all along that it was dangerous for you to be in charge of so much. You still lack the maturity to control your tongue and your temper. I was just waiting for the right man to come along with the right qualifications. And Mr. Purlee is the right man. Now there'll be no more discussion."

Before Mr. Purlee came to the factory, each day had been pure joy to Fred. Now it had changed to pure agony. The older man was curt and harsh when speaking to Sammy Joe. Fred could tell right away that the man held a dislike for black people.

At first, Fred and Sammy did just what they'd always done—firing up the steam engine and raising the pressure in the boilers until pistons were pumping, the flywheel was spinning, and the lathes upstairs were whirring and purring. But Edgar Purlee let them know right away, they were to do nothing—they were to *touch* nothing—until he gave the orders.

"Now, boy," Mr. Purlee said to Sammy Joe, "time to fill that first firebox. Open 'er up and get that coal in there."

"He's not a boy!" Fred stated, not bothering to hide the irritation in his voice. "He's older than I am."

Mr. Purlee turned around to look at Fred, his pig eyes narrowing. "Well, I guess that makes you *both* a couple of boys, then, don't it?" Turning back to where Sammy Joe was shoveling, he said, "It'll take more than that, boy. Put in another couple shovelsful."

"There're two fireboxes," Fred said, stepping forward. "No need to overload either one. They work in tandem."

Mr. Purlee whirled around. "I have eyes. I can see there are two fireboxes. I believe I remember your father telling me you were supposed to show respect to your new superintendent. If I hear anything else from you, I'll have to report your insolence to Mr. Allerton."

Sammy Joe looked over at Fred, his eyes wide, his black face shiny and dripping with perspiration. Fred gave a shrug and turned away. The anger burning in his midsection was hotter than the inside of that firebox. He had never, nor would he ever, call Sammy Joe "boy."

Over the past two years, he'd watched Sammy Joe's progress, not only in his education, but in his knowledge and appreciation of the steam engine as well. Fred saw Sammy Joe as highly intelligent and very tenderhearted—sort of like Damon. Unfortunately it was obvious that Mr. Purlee did not share Fred's views.

That night at the meeting of abolitionists at Mr. Chase's house, the discussion centered around strategic people in the city who were known to assist slave catchers.

"Over the past few years," Mr. Chase explained, "those who come into town hunting for escaped slaves know right where to go for assistance. It's good for us to know who those contacts are as best we can. 'He who is forewarned is forearmed,' as the saying goes."

Tim added, "We've found it's most usually businessmen who have much to gain from favor from the southern states."

Fred knew his own father had much to gain from favor from the South, since his largest accounts were in the Deep South. But Papa would never assist a slave catcher.

Tonight the quiet Quaker Levi Coffin was attending the meeting. Mr. Coffin and his wife, Catharine, had probably secreted more slaves to freedom through their work with the Underground Railroad than any other people alive. He'd come to Cincinnati from Indiana last year, thinking his work with the railroad was over, but it had barely begun.

Brother Coffin, as he was called, was in agreement with Chase's comments, but added, "We must never forget that while *men* may assist the slave catchers, *God* helps us to hide the desperate runaways." The smooth-shaven Coffin sat straight in his chair and looked at those in the room with gentle eyes. "Remaining forever aware of God's power will ward off fear and anger. Jesus' death and atonement were for the slave catcher and those who assist them, just as much as for thee and for me."

Then he looked right at Fred, almost as though he sensed the turmoil roiling inside of him. Fred had to look away from those kind eyes.

Fred held Brother Coffin in high esteem, as did the others in the group. Even Salmon Chase submitted to Brother Coffin. Always garbed in plain gray, the man had been instrumental in raising up groups of small farmers throughout the South who did not own slaves.

Together with the abolitionist William Lloyd Garrison, he'd opened a store at Sixth and Elm, a store that sold free-labor goods. Fred had been in the store many times, picking up bundles of pamphlets to distribute. How this man—who'd seen so much injustice, hate, and prejudice—could be so full of love was more than Fred could comprehend.

Following the meeting, as Fred was walking toward home beside Tim, he decided to confide in his cousin about Edgar Purlee. He even told Tim about Edgar's rough treatment of Sammy Joe. When Fred finished, Tim pulled out a notepad and a pencil from his pocket. Pausing beneath a gas lamp, he said, "Give me the man's name again."

"Edgar Purlee," Fred said, spelling the last name.

"And your papa said he was from where?"

"Pittsburgh. He said Mr. Purlee had worked with steam engines in the mills there."

Tim nodded and put the pad away. "Your papa means well, Fred. I've known Ben for years, and he has a good heart. He's hired this man because he thinks it's best for all concerned."

Fred couldn't see that. He couldn't see past the awful feelings of being betrayed. "Why did you take down his name?"

"In my business, I look for strangers in the city. Especially strangers who are hateful to a black person." Tim gave a wry smile. "I guess I'm getting cynical and wary, Fred. I'm not as trusting as Brother Coffin."

"Nor am I," Fred added. "Nor am I." And he didn't trust Edgar Purlee one bit, either.

Fred quickly learned that Edgar Purlee was forever in a foul mood. "Like a bear with a sore head," Sammy Joe said. Fred agreed. Purlee's surly manner affected the men on the lathes as well. Fred's ears alone heard the grumbling and complaining among the workers. Papa didn't know.

After the midday whistle was blown, Fred would close himself in his small anteroom, pull out a good book, and read in peace. He had two new books on railroad locomotives.

Sometimes he worked with his batteries and the electricity; but after he'd moved all the chemicals out, he found that having part of the equipment at home and part at the factory wasn't working out at all. Many of the chemicals were needed for the experiments with electricity.

The laboratory at home now had two windows and the door was hung. Fred thought perhaps he'd take the rest of the equipment home as well. One evening after they were off work, he and Sammy Joe were walking up the hill on John Street. They often walked partway together before Sammy Joe turned west toward Little Africa, as his area of town was called.

As they walked along, Fred asked Sammy Joe if he would help pack up the rest of Fred's laboratory equipment.

"You don't trust Mr. Purlee?" Sammy Joe asked.

"That's part of it. But I want to have the equipment all together. I have a lab at home now."

Sammy Joe nodded. Off in the distance they heard the sound of a train locomotive coming into the station. "Fred, what do you suppose a body's gotta know to work on that old locomotive?"

Fred shrugged. "Not much more than what it takes to work on a stationary steam engine, I suppose."

"That's what I think, too. Wonder if they're needing help."

"Sammy Joe, you're not thinking about leaving, are you?"

"Ain't never thought nothing of the sort before now."

"Before Mr. Purlee."

"I don't mind that he calls me boy. I don't mind that he talks mean. But there's something else."

"What?"

Sammy Joe just shook his head. "Can't rightly say. But I

don't like the way he looks at me. It just doesn't feel right."

"Different than how he looks at me?" Fred had to admit he hadn't noticed. But then, he'd not lived with hate the way Sammy Joe had.

"It's different, all right."

The long low whistle sounded from the area of the train station. Fred glanced over in that direction. "Sammy Joe, you just do what you know is right for you. I'll understand."

"I know you will, Fred." And he loped off toward home.

Papa spent long hours at his furniture factory. He arrived early and stayed late. The next morning, when Fred came inside the front door, Papa was standing there waiting for him.

"Come up to my office," he said solemnly. Fred dutifully followed him up the stairs and through the accounting area into Papa's office. There sat Edgar Purlee. His eyes were narrowed, his soft fleshy face set in a scowl. The beard appeared more frowsy than ever.

Papa closed the door.

"You!" Mr. Purlee growled. "You set that trap for me. You could have killed me."

Fred was stupefied. "What trap?"

"That metal plate in that little room. It liked to have killed me," he said, rubbing his forearm.

Fred bit his tongue to stifle the laughter. So. Mr. Purlee had touched his electrical rat killer and received a shock! Well, good for him!

CHAPTER 7
Julia's New Friend

"Fred," Papa said, "I've warned you about leaving danger-ous materials about where people can get hurt."

"I didn't leave it about," Fred replied, straining to keep the laughter from sounding in his voice. "It was in my labo-ratory, and the door was closed."

Edgar Purlee looked at Papa. "Am I or am I not superin-tendent over the entire area?"

"I gave you jurisdiction over the entire area," Papa assured him.

Mr. Purlee turned to Fred, giving him a look of disdain. "I happened to have been looking for a tool."

"No tools that have to do with the steam engine are kept in

my laboratory," Fred said, his voice growing tighter. "That's my private room."

Papa glared at Fred with a warning look in his eyes. It told Fred he was close to getting himself in more trouble. He'd have to watch his words.

"Unless you've forgotten," Papa said sternly, "this is still my factory."

"Yes, sir."

"All the rest of your equipment will be out of here by tomorrow morning."

"Yes, sir."

"That's all. You may go."

Fred stood to leave. "May I leave a few books here?"

"A few books," Papa agreed. "But that's all."

As Fred went back downstairs, he wondered how Papa would like it when all of a sudden the rat population increased once again. The electrical rat killer had been doing away with about one rat each night. Sometimes two.

When he told Sammy Joe the story of the shock that Mr. Purlee took, they had a good laugh together.

"I can see him now," Sammy Joe said. "Jumping around like a snake bit him." He shook his head as laughter overtook him. "That electrical contraption, it does a fine job—some rats it kills, some rats it only shocks."

When Mr. Purlee came down the stairs and heard their laughter, he was angrier than ever. Both Sammy Joe and Fred attempted to sidestep him the remainder of that day.

Late that Saturday afternoon, when Fred went to Brother Coffin's store to pick up pamphlets to distribute, Sister Catharine came up to him. "Good day, Master Allerton. I trust thou art faring well."

Like her husband, Mrs. Coffin wore clothing of plain Quaker gray, with a small white cap over her bun, tied in a neat bow beneath her chin.

Fred nodded and tipped his cap. "I'm fine, thank you."

She took him to the back room, where magazines, books, newspapers, and pamphlets were lying about in neat organized stacks. She handed him a bundle. "Your cousin Timothy left a message for thee. Thou art to stop by his office this afternoon." Her voice was as quiet and gentle as her husband's.

"Tim wants to talk to me?" Fred adjusted the heavy bundle under his arm.

She nodded and smiled. "He acted as though it were important."

Fred tipped his hat again, thanking her, and hurried outside to go to Tim's office, which was just down the street. The May sunshine was just hot enough to cause the piles of horse droppings in the street to put off a strong aroma. It wasn't quite as bad in his neighborhood, where the traffic wasn't so thick. Here in the heart of the city, it was terrible.

Past the book bindery, Shillito's Dry Goods, and Harrison's Hardware, Fred walked. Then he turned in at the eight-story Carlisle building, which housed a number of offices. He approached the door with the words "Salmon P. Chase, Attorney at Law" scrolled in black on the frosted glass pane. Fred tapped at the door, and Tim answered. "Ah, there you are, Frederick. Come on in. I've something to tell you."

"Now? Before the pamphlets are distributed?" Usually, Fred was instructed to get the pamphlets out just as quickly as possible.

"Yes, now," Tim replied.

Fred followed through the outer offices into a small corner office that was strewn about with more books and papers than Fred had ever seen. And Papa thought Fred's laboratory was a mess. It couldn't compare to this.

Tim cleaned off a chair and waved Fred toward it. Fred put his bundle on the floor and pulled the chair closer to Tim's desk. Sitting down on the other side of his desk, Tim pulled out a piece of paper and waved it in the air. "We've done a little scouting, Fred, and we've learned something about Mr. Edgar Purlee."

Fred leaned forward. "You did?" He could hardly believe that Tim would have taken the trouble.

"We think Purlee's in cahoots somehow with a group of southern organizers." He looked at the paper in his hand. "In Pittsburgh, Edgar Purlee led an attack on the home of a man who was active in the abolitionist movement. They were successful in burning the house to the ground. Thankfully, both the man and his wife escaped unharmed."

Fred's heart sped up a beat. "Purlee did that? What's he doing in Cincinnati?"

Tim shook his head. "No way of knowing just yet. We'll have to keep an eye on him. We're spreading the word among all the workers—especially those, like Brother and Sister Coffin, who actually assist the runaways."

Fred's mouth went dry. Why did Papa have to be so blind about such things?

"Didn't you mention working with a black man at the factory?" Tim asked.

"Yes. Sammy Joe's a good worker. He understands that engine almost as well as I do." Fred swallowed hard. "You don't think Sammy Joe's in any danger, do you?"

"As long as money-hungry slave catchers have all the freedom in the world to take whomever they want back to the slave owners, no black man in Cincinnati is safe."

"But Sammy Joe's free. He's educated."

Tim exhaled a long sigh. "I wish that made a difference, Frederick. We've repealed the black laws, but no-account slave catchers still get away with kidnapping free black men and women."

"What do you want me to do?"

"Watch and listen. If you see this Mr. Purlee about town, report his whereabouts to the group."

Fred picked up his bundle and stood to go. "I'll do whatever you need me to do," he said.

"Try not to stir up trouble with this man," Tim warned.

Fred smiled. "I think it's too late for that. I already have."

Fred took the pamphlets around to the stagecoach office, the library, down to the landing to the ticket offices of the steamboat lines, then over to the train station. He always made the train station the last on the list. That way his hands were empty and he could pick up scrap metal. And, of course, if there was extra time, he talked to the workers.

Today there were men working on the tracks. "Hey there," he said. "Does the CH&D hire black folk to work on the locomotives?"

A tall thin man straightened up from where he was bent over his work. He pulled off his sweat-stained slouch hat and scratched his head. "I don't rightly think they hire them to work on the locomotives, but there's lots of repair work to do. Sometimes we ride the train out to where the work needs to be done."

Sammy Joe would like that. Fred nodded. "Thank you, sir," he said. After scouring the tracks for pieces of metal, he turned toward home. As he walked along, he thought about what the man had said. Working on the railroad sounded like a great adventure. He'd longed to ride a train for years.

Maybe he and Sammy Joe could both sign on with the C H & D. What a relief it would be to get away from Edgar Purlee.

Later, as he approached his own house, Fred saw Julia out on the front walk playing skip rope with a friend. Her broken arm was all healed and giving her no trouble.

Most girls Julia's age played "cradle" or "high-waters low-waters"—and not too high at that. But not Fred's sister. The girls had tied one end of the rope to the front wrought iron fence and the friend was twirling the other end. Julia was doing "overs and unders" with all the agility of an athletic boy.

"Hello, Fred!" she called out when she saw him. "Come and meet my new friend." Deftly, she hopped out of the twirling rope.

As Fred approached, he could see the friend was terribly shy. She appeared to want to dissolve into Julia's shadow. She could hardly force herself to look at Fred as Julia introduced them.

"Fred, this is my new friend, Henrietta. But she likes to be called Etta."

"Hello there, Etta," Fred said as politely as he could. "Do you have a last name?"

The girl ducked her head. "It's Purlee," she said.

Her voice was so soft, Fred was certain he'd misunderstood. "What was that again?"

"Purlee," Julia repeated. "She's new in my grade. She and her family moved here from Pittsburgh awhile back. Her mama let her come and play with me this afternoon."

But Fred had stopped listening. So this was the daughter of an abolitionist hater? "I best be getting inside to see what mama needs of me," he said, his voice suddenly turning cool. He tipped his cap and let himself in through the gate.

Later he'd have a talk with Julia and warn her about being friends with the likes of the Purlees.

That evening Fred waited until Julia went out to close up the henhouse and grabbed the opportunity to talk with her alone. He carefully explained that Etta was, in fact, the daughter of the man Papa had hired—the man who was causing him terrible problems at the factory and who assisted slave catchers.

Julia walked about the yard and through Mama's garden, which was sporting precise rows of new green shoots of vegetables. "Shoo, chick, chick, chick. Shoo now." The chickens cackled and ran before her as she waved her hands to herd them into the henhouse. The spring evening was cool, and she hadn't even grabbed her shawl or bonnet. Julia was like that.

"So," he said, following along behind her and rounding up a few of the strays, "you'll want to be careful about the friends you choose. These are dangerous times we live in. Why, even Sammy Joe's life could be in danger because of this man."

Julia said nothing as she shooed the rest of the chickens into the henhouse and closed and bolted the door. When she came back to where Fred was standing, he said, "Julia, didn't you hear a word I said? This is important!"

"Frederick Allerton, you may be my older brother, but you don't know everything."

"I know about Edgar Purlee."

"But you don't know about his daughter. Etta's a nice girl who needs a friend." Julia turned and headed toward the back porch. "And I'll very well choose my *own* friends if you don't mind," she called over her shoulder.

Fred stood there staring at Julia's back as she disappeared

into the house. He heaved a sigh. What was the use? Papa wouldn't listen. Now Julia wouldn't listen. He stepped inside his laboratory, which still held the rich aroma of new wood. He lit the lantern and hung it on a nail on the wall. This place had become his sanctuary.

He'd barely started working on an experiment with his two big batteries when he thought he heard a buggy stop out front. Taking the lantern, he went around the side of the house to see Dr. Henry Lankford stepping down from his buggy. The young, long-legged doctor, only a few years younger than Timothy, had recently graduated from medical school and was working closely with old Dr. Logan.

"Dr. Lankford. Hello," Fred said. "This isn't a professional visit I hope."

"Evening, Frederick." Not answering the question, he asked, "Is your papa at home?"

"He came in just a short while ago. Come around to the back door. I'm sure Mama has a pot of coffee on."

As he lifted the lantern to guide the way, Fred could see that the young doctor's face was grim.

Once inside, Mama bade him sit down at the kitchen table. Meg came in from the front room, where she'd been sewing. She kept to herself a great deal of late. Papa brought a mug for Dr. Lankford, and Mama filled it to the brim with her strong black coffee.

"*Hefeküchen*?" Mama asked. "Fresh baked today."

The young doctor had removed his hat, and a shock of blond hair fell across his forehead. "Just coffee, thank you."

Papa blew across the top of his steaming mug. "Tell us what brings you to our home this evening, Henry."

Dr. Lankford shifted in his chair. "I wanted you folks to know right away so you could be prepared," he began.

"Prepared?" Papa asked. "For what?"

"Cholera has been reported in the city."

Fred watched as Mama's face turned ashen. "No," she whispered. "Dear God, not again."

CHAPTER 8

Cholera!

It was as though the air in the kitchen froze for a moment. No one moved. Fred had heard stories of the terrifying disease. It spread quickly and people died quickly. The fear in Mama's face was nearly as frightening as the thought of the disease. He'd heard how—due to the awful diarrhea, vomiting, and violent cramps—the body dehydrated. Without treatment, a person could die within hours. The epidemic usually hit worst in the poorer sections of town.

"I've done a great deal of study about this disease," Dr. Lankford told them. "Some physicians are now beginning to call it the 'water disease.' Evidence is fairly strong that the contamination is in the water. You folks have your own cistern, do you not?"

Papa nodded. Mama said, "Yes, our own cistern out back."

"It would be best if you drank no other water for a time. Just to be sure."

They nodded, no one saying much.

"We're learning more about the need for sanitation," the doctor went on. "Some people won't listen to what we have to say in this area, but I knew you folks would be different."

"What should we do?" Papa's voice was raspy.

"Order a barrel of lime from the mercantile. Keep a bucket at the privy, and every night pour about half a bucketful of the powdered lime on the waste."

Papa nodded.

"What does the lime do?" Julia wanted to know.

Fred looked over at his little sister. She seemed to be the only one in the room unaffected by the news. Perhaps she didn't grasp the seriousness of the matter. Mama always said Julia looked at the world through rose-colored glasses.

"Lime, we've learned, causes waste to break down faster and tends to keep flies from breeding there." Dr. Lankford cupped his hands about his mug and stared into it. "We'll be working with the city council to attempt to have ordinances passed to forbid waste dumping in the streets. The streets need to be cleaned and lime spread there as well. Funds must be allocated for this to be done on a regular basis."

"Will the city leaders agree?" Meg asked softly.

"I don't know. We can only hope." Dr. Lankford looked at Papa. "Ben, I'd like to ask you to attend the next council meeting and help us get these ordinances passed."

"What good could I do?" Papa asked.

"Not much by yourself. But if you stand with others, you can do a great deal."

Dr. Lankford sounded almost like Salmon Chase, Fred thought. Fred knew it was true. He'd seen the results of people all across the North joining hands to help the enslaved blacks. The same method could work in cleaning up the city to prevent the spread of this terrible disease. Papa wasn't much inclined to get involved—he kept pretty much to himself. However, to Fred's surprise, Papa agreed.

"I'll be there," he said.

Dr. Lankford finished his coffee, then stood to leave. "One more thing. Always empty the chamber pots into the privy. Never in the yard or street. And use the lime every day. You can encourage your neighbors to do the same."

Mama nodded. "Whatever you say, we will do, Doctor."

"We'll be printing these instructions in the newspapers as well. With God's help, we'll get the word out and educate the people."

"Would that it had been done before the awful cholera came," Mama said.

"Yes, Emma," the doctor replied, "but sad to say, most people don't listen unless there's a calamity."

Papa showed Dr. Lankford out the front door.

"Well," Meg said softly, stroking Goldie, who lay in her lap, "it appears that Damon and the Hendrickses left just in time."

The mercantile delivered the barrel of lime the very next day, and it became Fred's job to take care of liming the privy.

He confided to Sammy Joe, "Papa trusts me with the privy, but not with my own steam engine." Fred couldn't imagine how things could get worse.

The entire family was anxious to hear from the Hendrickses, but of course Meg was more anxious than all of them to hear news of her beloved Damon. They'd already harvested two messes of English peas from Mama's garden in late May before the first letters arrived. There was a main letter written in part by Aunt Lucy and Susannah and a private letter from Damon to Meg.

Mama suggested the family gather in the parlor to read the main letter together, but they had to wait for Papa to come home. Meg went to her room alone with her letter. By the time Papa did arrive, Julia was fit to be tied. Mama kept scolding her and telling her to stop bouncing around, but it did no good.

Julia called upstairs for Meg to come down and join them. When she did, Meg's eyes were red—just as they'd been the weeks after Damon had left. It made Fred upset at Damon all over again for hurting Meg so.

Julia insisted on reading the letter from the Hendrickses aloud. In it, Aunt Lucy told of purchasing their team of oxen and wagon in St. Louis and, just as planned, loading them on the steamboat to Independence, Missouri.

"We were deeply thankful for having that foreknowledge," she wrote, "for in St. Louis we paid about half of the asking price in Independence." The letter, dated in mid-April, continued:

We are waiting now. Waiting for what? Grass. Can you imagine that? We've learned if the wagons leave too early, the grass isn't tall enough for the animals to graze along the way. It's better, we're told, to wait for the grass than to try to take so much grain along the way.

The next part of the letter was written by Susannah and

described the scene of the camps outside Independence:

> *Papa says the area is a full three miles square,
> and every inch is filled with wagons, livestock,
> and families. You never saw so much dust in all
> your born days. When there is no wind, the skies
> are filled clouds of gray dust hanging in the air.*
>
> *But worse than the choking dust is the noise.
> You can just about imagine what all this "gather-
> ing" must sound like. Cincinnati's public landing
> is quieter than this place.*

Julia looked up from the letter. "I can almost see the place. Can't you?" She read on.

> *Mama and I have become tolerable campfire
> cooks. At least both Stephen and Papa have been
> kind enough to say so. I told them they'd better
> like it since they'll be eating it for several months
> to come.*
>
> *People here hail from all parts of the country. I
> met a girl from New York City. Her father is cer-
> tain he will find gold and strike it rich. She told
> me all the pretty things she plans to purchase
> when they get rich. The first time her father
> hitched up his team of oxen, he ran the wagon
> right into a tree. Stephen and Papa tried not to
> laugh. But we could sympathize since both
> Stephen and Papa found it a strenuous trial in
> learning to work with a team of oxen.*

Fred tried to imagine what it would be like to handle a

team of strong oxen. He'd handled a team of horses many times when Papa rented a livery for deliveries to the dock. But oxen? That would be a different story.

Stephen and I named our two oxen Esau and Jacob. They're gentle as kittens. Much nicer than the dumb old mules that some folk have purchased to pull their wagons. We saw a man get bit right in the backside by his own mule. He let out a yowl that carried all through the camp. Again, we tried not to laugh. Esau and Jacob are gentlemen and have much better manners.

Julia stopped to chuckle over that part of the letter. "The next part is in Aunt Lucy's writing again," she informed them.

John has purchased all our supplies now. We have nearly two hundred pounds of flour, one hundred fifty pounds of bacon, ten pounds of coffee, twenty pounds of sugar, and ten pounds of salt. It seems so very much right now, but we know the journey will be long and every bit will be needed. I'm wondering if there will be room in the wagon for us.

We've been writing parts of this letter over several days, planning to send it just before we leave. John says we're leaving with a group tomorrow morning. Pray for us. Our thoughts are with you and we miss you all terribly. We all send our love.

Turning the letter so all of them could see, Julia pointed

at the bottom, where they had all signed their names. The letter had been posted nearly a month ago. Fred figured the Hendrickses were probably midway through Nebraska Territory by now. While it was good to receive the letter, it served only to remind Fred of how much he missed all of them. Including Damon.

CHAPTER 9
Meg's New Work

As the warm days of spring turned into the hot days of summer, Fred spent more and more time in his laboratory. He strung wire from his laboratory up to Julia's room, climbing up on the porch roof to secure it. In her room, he set up a makeshift telegraph, just like he'd seen illustrated in his science books. In his laboratory building, he set up the sending apparatus.

The first couple nights he worked on it, Julia called out the window saying, "Nothing! It's not making a peep."

He wasn't sure if the problem was in the batteries, in the wiring, or in the apparatus itself, but he kept on working.

Finally one evening after dark, Julia suddenly stuck her head out her bedroom window. "It's clicking, Fred!" she exclaimed. "Your telegraph is clicking. Now when are you going to teach me the Morse code so I can understand what you're saying?"

Fred had been working on that very thing. He'd been teaching himself the code and had it almost learned by heart. Now he'd teach Julia.

When Julia told Papa the next morning about the success of the experiment, he simply said, "So what good is that? The two of you can talk to one another any time." Papa couldn't see how important it was to Fred that he'd made the whole contraption work. Papa just didn't understand.

With the coming of summer, the number of reported cases of cholera increased. Each day the newspapers carried the rising numbers. The newsboys on the corners in downtown Cincinnati cried out the figures. "Extra! Extra! Read all about it! Cholera kills fifty more Cincinnatians!" they would shout. Their calls of news each day struck fear into the hearts of all who heard. And the numbers kept climbing.

One evening as Fred was coming home from the factory, he saw Meg walking along the street up ahead of him. The fringe of her shawl fluttered in the breeze as she walked quickly along. Her parasol and flowered bonnet protected her face from the late afternoon sun. She'd probably been out calling.

"Meg," he called out. "Wait."

She turned about, her skirts sweeping the street as she did so. "Hello, Fred. I didn't expect to see you."

Catching up with her, he said, "Where've you been? Don't you usually do your calling in the mornings, when it's not so warm?"

"I haven't been on a social call," she said.

That was a vague statement. "If Mama needed something from the store, I could have done it."

"I wasn't at the store, either."

"Well, pray tell, where have you been?"

"Dr. Lankford's office."

Fred came to a sudden halt. "You're not sick!"

She shook her head. "I'm fine, Fred. I wish you weren't asking. I was going to tell the family at supper. I've volunteered my services to Dr. Lankford."

"You what?" Fred felt sick to his stomach. "Margaret, you've done some crazy things in your time, but that's about the most addle-headed thing I've ever heard of. You can't go near those sick people! You just can't."

"I'm no good to anyone if I sit around the house pining for Damon. I've received the letter I'd been longing for. Now I know I'll not hear from him again until autumn. I must keep busy."

Meg was always so precise. So quiet. So determined. It infuriated Fred. He was so angry he could hardly speak. "Well, I'll talk to Mama and Papa. We'll all stop you. They'll never allow you to do such a lamebrained thing."

But he knew, looking at her quiet face, that it was useless. He took off and ran all the way home, shutting himself in his laboratory until after dark. His whole world seemed to be falling apart around him, and there was nothing he could do about any of it.

That night at supper, Papa and Mama both tried to talk Meg out of following through on her plans, but she was adamant. Meg chose to work with those Over-the-Rhine who were ill. "Where 'our people' are," she said. Mama's sisters and their families lived in Germantown, on the other side of the Ohio and Erie Canal, which all Cincinnatians called the "Rhine." Oma Schiller was there as well.

Papa and Mama looked at each other with understanding.

"All right, Meg," Papa said. "Do what you think is best."

Fred stared down at his plate. Would anything ever go right again?

Each working day became interminably long for Fred as he turned over all his responsibilities to Mr. Purlee. One week, Papa took him out of the basement altogether and set him to work in the accounting department. Fred couldn't keep his mind on the work for worrying about Sammy Joe and about the steam engine.

Jesse, the head accountant, became quite exasperated as he tried to clean up the messes that Fred made in the books. "I don't think you're cut out to be an accountant," he said, shaking his head.

"Tell Papa that," Fred said sharply.

The next week Fred was upstairs with the woodcarvers, cabinetmakers, and finishers. These men were adept at hand carving solid wood. They created motifs of shells and scrolls. They also carved out leaf designs, urns and flames, and the claw-and-ball foot. The room was crowded with pieces of furniture, from small chairs to massive sideboards weighing several hundred pounds. Wood shavings and sawdust were everywhere, and the good aromas of wood never abated.

While Fred admired the sculptured beauty and enjoyed watching these craftsmen work, the men knew not to trust any detailed work to him. Mostly he did sanding and finishing. Sometimes they let him screw on the brass knobs and drawer handles.

Papa continually told Fred that he must know every facet of the business. Fred wanted to tell Papa that he wasn't interested in every facet of the business, but he was trying not to talk back. Occasionally he was assigned to once again return to the basement and help Sammy Joe, but it wasn't the same.

"Why are the gauges steamed over?" Fred demanded of Mr. Purlee one morning. "I can't even read these things."

"A gauge serves little purpose when you know what the engine is doing," Edgar snapped. "And I know what the engine is doing."

"The gauges are installed for a distinct purpose. The machine was designed to have the gauges to measure the pressure. Nothing is foolproof."

"Are you saying you don't trust this steam engine?" There was an unmistakable taunt in Purlee's voice that grated on Fred's nerves.

"I *did* trust it, but not anymore."

Sammy Joe watched the two of them with fear in his eyes.

"I take it you mean since I came," Purlee shot back.

"You can take it any way you want."

"Your father said you're to show me respect as your superior. If you don't like what I'm doing, why don't you take it up with him?"

"I believe I will!" Fred knew he had to get out of that hot steamy basement before his own fuse blew. Taking the stairs two at a time, he barged into Papa's office without even knocking.

"That machine down there is designed with safety features, one of which are gauges that need to be read every hour or so. But now the gauges are so steamed over a person can't even read them. So what's the use of even having them on there if they can't be seen?" Fred was ranting, and he knew it. But he just couldn't stop the volcano inside him from erupting.

Papa looked up calmly from the work on his desk. "So

unsteam them. What's all this fuss and clamor about?"

"Your Mr. Purlee doesn't seem to think they need to be *unsteamed*." What a silly word—unsteamed. His Papa hadn't an inkling of how the steam engine even worked.

"Then I trust Mr. Purlee knows what he's talking about. He's worked with more and bigger steam engines than we have here."

"So you're going to take his side in the matter?"

"Frederick, I am not taking sides. I hired Mr. Purlee to do a job, and he's doing it."

Fred struggled to keep his wits about him. Uninvited, he sat down in the chair nearest his father's desk. "Papa, your superintendent, Edgar Purlee, is a man who assists slave catchers. Did you know that? When the slave catchers come into town, they know they can go to him for help. Sometimes he puts them on the trail of runaway slaves. Back in Pittsburgh, Purlee led an attack on the home of a couple who helped runaway slaves."

"Unless you are prepared to prove those allegations in a court of law, young man, I don't want to hear another word. I don't hire people on the basis of their actions outside this factory or their beliefs."

Fred stood now, knowing nothing he said would make any difference to his father. It was senseless to continue talking. But he added, "You keep saying that you want me to learn every facet of this business, but you don't know every facet yourself."

"Must I remind you, I never wanted that infernal machine in my factory to begin with?"

"No," Fred said. "No need to remind me. You've never let me forget it for a moment." With that, he slammed out of the office.

Never had he spoken to his father in such a tone. And it made him feel more wretched than he'd ever felt in his life. Why couldn't he bridle his tongue as he'd been told to?

Just when he thought nothing could get any worse, that evening Fred learned there were *two* Purlee daughters. And both of them were at his house!

CHAPTER 10
Attorney Ward Baker

Though Fred wasn't home much, he knew Julia was spending more and more time with Etta Purlee, because when he *was* home, Julia talked of little else but her new friend. Summer meant there were free days in which the girls could do things together.

According to Julia, when she met Etta's sixteen-year-old sister, Molly, she just *knew* Molly and Meg would become good friends as well. And thus two Purlee girls came visiting instead of one.

The four girls were on the front porch drinking lemonade and sewing when Fred arrived home that afternoon. Had he known who was there when he approached, he might have gone around the block and slipped in over the back fence.

But he stumbled right into the foursome unawares.

"Fred," Julia said in her ever-perky voice, "I want you to meet Molly Purlee, Etta's older sister. She's going to be helping Meg with the work with Dr. Lankford."

Fred touched his hat, but didn't step over to shake her hand. "Pleased to meet you," he mumbled.

Molly was more attractive than her younger sister and not nearly as shy. She had a turned-up nose and rosy cheeks, and though her long sandy hair was fastened back in a coiled braid, tiny tendrils escaped and curled softly about her face. Goldie was curled up contentedly in the girl's lap. Fred couldn't keep himself from wondering how such a wretched man as Edgar Purlee could have such a pretty daughter.

He started to go inside when Julia asked, "Will you be home tonight, Fred? Can we show the girls how your telegraph works?"

Fred was sure he'd never want to show his telegraph to two daughters of an overt pro-slavery man. Who knew what they might tell their father?

"I'm going to the city council meeting with Papa." Then he added in a firm voice. "Afterward I might meet with all my *abolitionist* friends."

Of course he wasn't meeting with them. He just wanted to make sure Molly Purlee knew where he stood. Satisfied, he went inside.

Fred and Papa walked from their home to city hall in silence. Fred wondered why it had always been so much easier to talk to Uncle John and Stephen. Or Damon. Or even Cousin Tim. Somehow that didn't seem right.

The city council meeting was heated. Not only was it a warm evening, but many people didn't agree with or believe in the measures the doctors were requesting. Everyone wanted to have his say. Some council members felt that the cost of city street cleanup was way over what the budget could handle. Others said that the measures would do no good—that nothing could stop the onslaught of the dread disease.

Dr. Logan—a man well respected by most everyone in the city—finally talked sense to the noisy group. "What is the price of a human life?" he asked the crowd. He reminded them of the scientific studies of Dr. Daniel Drake during the 1832 epidemic.

"Perhaps if we had budgeted funds to take care of the sanitation needs of this city seventeen years ago, there might not be another epidemic upon us now."

Fred found himself wishing he'd read more about this subject so he could enter into the lively discussion. As it was, he knew very little except for what Dr. Lankford had told them.

Dr. Lankford also spoke and revealed new studies that pointed to the fact that there was a direct correlation between the presence of filth and the spread of disease. "We certainly don't know all there is to know about the matter," he said, "but we know that much. Doesn't it make sense to follow through with action on what we know to be true?"

The hour was late when a vote was finally taken. To Fred's great relief, the councilors voted to approve funds to begin street cleanup.

At the next abolitionist meeting, a special guest was in attendance. The tall, gray-haired black man, Ward Baker, served as a university professor in Canada, in addition to being an attorney there. His many published pamphlets, which described the successful growing black communities in Canada, found their way deep into the South, where slaves learned what freedom had to offer them. Fred had read many of Attorney Baker's writings and found them to be intelligent, powerful, and concise works.

The black attorney had once lived in Cincinnati. Many times Fred had been told the story of how Tim, as a young boy, saved Ward's life. Tim had compelled his father, Richard Allerton, to help rescue Ward and his family just before a riot broke out in Little Africa. Every time Tim told the story, it made Fred respect his cousin even more.

The windows of the Chase parlor were thrown wide open, the tapestry drapes drawn back, and a weak summer breeze floated through the stuffy room.

"We're honored to have you in our presence," Mr. Chase told Ward as the meeting got underway, "but you've arrived at a rather unfortunate time." He was referring, of course, to the cholera cases that were growing in number each day.

Ward assured them he wasn't going to be in the area long enough to catch the cholera. He'd come specifically to see Tim, to report on the growth of the communities in Canada, and to discuss improvements in the way the Underground Railroad was being operated.

Turning to Brother Coffin, Ward said, "Your name is almost revered in our area. Scores of our citizens owe their freedom to you and your work. They remember your kindness as well as your daring."

Brother Coffin only smiled. "I'm a very small cog in a very large wheel," he said modestly.

But Fred knew that wasn't true. The man was a legend. The pro-slavery people hated him. Fred tried to imagine all those happy black people in the Canadian communities, living in freedom from fear for the first time in their lives. He thought of those people who'd said that blacks were not people at all and that they were incapable of the ability to learn or to govern themselves. What ridiculous statements, and yet so many chose to believe them.

The evening was a memorable one for Fred. Following the meeting, as he shook the broad, strong hand of Ward Baker, he felt as though he were touching a part of history.

"You favor your cousin Timothy a great deal," Ward said to Fred. "It warms my heart to know that you are following in his footsteps."

"Frederick here designed and built a steam engine all by himself," Tim put in, making Fred blush. "The engine drives lathes in his father's furniture factory. He's even rigged up his own telegraph in his laboratory at home. And it works!" Fred was astonished at the pride in Tim's voice.

Ward smiled, showing his even white teeth. "A son to be proud of."

Neither Tim nor Fred told him any differently. Fred wished he truly were a son to be proud of. Instead he'd have to be content to be a cousin to be proud of.

As Tim and Fred walked home together following the meeting, Fred asked Tim many questions about Ward Baker. The tone of Tim's voice let him know the level of respect he held for the black attorney. "He taught me by word and example how to care about others, how to not become bitter or angry, and most of all, how to trust God."

Fascinated as Fred was about Ward Baker, Tim's words were a bitter pill to swallow when his feelings against Papa and Edgar Purlee were so judgmental. Fred saw no way that he could ever forgive Papa for treating him so unjustly.

Meg was up when Fred arrived home. He was glad to find her alone. Meg didn't talk much these days. He knew her heart and life were empty without Damon.

Fred had tried every way he knew of to convince her to cease her work with Dr. Lankford, but to no avail. Daily, she went into the German community to assist. "I'm becoming a pretty good nurse," she'd say to Fred. The conversation would be closed.

This night as Fred came in the back door, Meg was sitting at the kitchen table with her sketchbook open. On the table stood a cut-glass vase filled with summer daisies and black-eyed Susans. Strewn around on the table were pastel charcoals and pages filled with her drawings. Fred was so proud of Meg's artistic abilities, he could scarcely believe he'd ever teased her about them.

She jumped up when he entered. "There you are. Mama had me put a plate of pork and kraut in the warming oven. I'll get it for you."

Fred rinsed his hands at the basin. "Were you with Dr. Lankford today?"

"I was. And will continue to be."

"Is it. . .Is it bad?"

She nodded as she set his plate on the table and filled his coffee mug. "Lots of people are dying, Fred. The Lord is teaching me how to comfort them just before they die. It's a sacred responsibility He's given me."

Fred didn't much like to talk about death and dying. It seemed he had enough to worry about without a terrifying epidemic sweeping through the city.

Meg sat back down to her sketching. Goldie was curled at her feet.

"Did Molly go with you?" Fred wanted to know.

Meg nodded. "She's becoming an efficient nurse as well. Dr. Lankford is proud of her."

Fred bowed his head and returned thanks for his food, just in case Meg was ready to scold him about forgetting. Then he said, "Meg, you know her father assists the slave catchers who come into town, don't you?"

"I believe Julia mentioned something about that."

"I don't see how you can compromise like this—dealing with those who believe the opposite of how we believe."

"Opposite of how *you* believe, Fred. You have no idea how I believe."

Fred stopped eating and looked at his sister. "I know you want to see slavery abolished. You don't want runaway slaves to be captured and returned to the bullwhips and chains. And you don't want free blacks to be kidnapped and taken into slavery against their will."

Meg put down the piece of lemon-colored charcoal she'd been working with and looked intently into Fred's eyes. "I want to see a young girl learn how to minister love and mercy to dying people, Fred. When Molly is giving a drink of water to someone burning with fever, not one dying person has asked her if she's pro-slavery or not. They have asked her to pray—and she does."

Meg's words cut Fred deeply. He stood to his feet and went off to bed. But sleep was a long time coming. Through his open window came the deep-throated whistle of a steamboat in the distance. How nice it would be to hop aboard and leave all this trouble and confusion behind.

CHAPTER 11
The Explosion

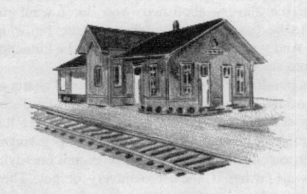

Summertime in the basement of the Allerton Furniture Factory felt about ten times hotter than the weather outside. The added heat worked to keep tempers on edge—both Fred's and Edgar Purlee's. There seemed to be no end to the number of times Fred got in trouble for talking back, especially whenever Edgar addressed Sammy Joe as "boy."

At one point Fred felt as though Papa didn't know what to do with him. Papa often told him to bridle his tongue.

One morning when Fred was on the first floor working on the lathes, oiling parts and inspecting, Alroy waved him over to where he was working.

"Aye, laddie, it was a sad day when that Purlee fellow ever set foot on this property," he said in his lilting Irish brogue. "The man's not fit to handle the job he's been given."

"Can't you tell Papa how you feel?" Fred asked.

"Nay, lad. He dinna hire me to be a-talkin', just a-workin'."

"Still, Papa trusts you, Alroy. As it is, Papa thinks *I'm* the problem, that I don't want to work under Purlee's authority."

Alroy shook his head. "More's the pity that the man can't see what's before his own two eyes God gave him."

"If Papa knew anything about the steam engine, he'd know Purlee wasn't doing a good job."

"Aye." Alroy waved his hand to indicate the other workers. "All we agree to that fact."

Fred stopped a moment. "What's that? Do you hear that noise?"

"What? All I hear's the lathe a-runnin'."

The noise came again, a little louder—a high squeal. Almost like a baby pig.

Suddenly Fred realized what was happening. It was the special signal he'd rigged.

"Clear this area!" Fred shouted, dropping his oilcan and running toward the stairs. Down the steps he bounded, two at a time. Mr. Purlee was standing at the gauges, squinting at them as though wishing he could see something.

"Sammy! She's gonna blow!" Fred yelled at the top of his voice.

Sammy was at the coal pile. He threw down his shovel and, with Fred, ran toward Edgar Purlee. They shoved Mr. Purlee into the corner and down to the floor and fell over him with their bodies. An explosion ripped through the ceiling up into the floor above. Hot steam spewed everywhere. Bits of wood and debris rained down on the three figures still huddled in the corner.

When it grew quiet, Fred looked up, expecting to see the heavy lathes ready to come falling down. But the hole wasn't all that large. It could have been much, much worse. The little water that was left in the boiler now dripped onto the floor.

"Get off me!" Edgar Purlee demanded, struggling to get up. His face was redder than Fred had ever seen it. "You rigged that. You did that on purpose. You're just trying to get me fired."

Fred had rigged it all right, but not in the way Mr. Purlee thought. Since the man was no longer using the gauges and Fred knew how dangerous that could be, Fred had slipped in one evening and rigged the whistle to act as a signal, just in case. It had worked. If the whistle hadn't sounded, Alroy and his partner would have been right above that hole. . . . Fred shivered at the thought.

He and Sammy Joe were on their feet quickly, looking over the damage. "Boiler's busted up pretty bad," Fred said to Sammy Joe.

"Overheated," Sammy Joe said to him softly. "I was trying to tell him. It wasn't any use."

Papa descended the stairs slowly, cautiously, his face pale, drawn, and tired looking. "Is everyone all right?" he asked.

Edgar scrambled to his feet and dusted off his trousers. Pointing to Fred, he said, "I'm all right, no thanks to him. That high-minded kid of yours rigged it to blow. I'll be hornswoggled if he didn't. He even knew the minute it was gonna go. Came running down here yelling to warn the boy there."

Purlee limped over to the stairway, squinting up at Ben Allerton. "Your son's hated me from the first minute I walked in this place. You know that's true. He's tried ten ways to Sunday to make me look bad, and now this. What are you gonna do about it?"

"Alroy," Papa called up through the hole.

Alroy's freckled face peered down through the ragged hole. "Sir?"

"You men come down here and help Sammy Joe clean up this mess." Turning to Fred he said, "You and Mr. Purlee come upstairs with me."

Fred stole a glance at Sammy Joe. Both of them knew they had saved Edgar Purlee's life. The man seemed to have no idea he'd fired the boiler up too hot.

Papa didn't let either of them speak. His mind was made up. "I'm closing down the steam engine for good," he said firmly. "I'm losing enough workers to cholera. I can't afford to blow the rest to smithereens."

Fred sat stone still as the words sunk in. No more steam engine. It was as though Papa had been waiting for just such an opportunity.

"I'll not take any more chances with the safety of my employees," Papa said. "It's too dangerous. Edgar, if you'd like to stay on, I'll make you supervisor over all the workers who run the hand-operated lathes."

Mr. Purlee nodded, rubbing his elbow, which had probably gotten smacked in the fall. "Suits me fine."

"And Sammy Joe?" Fred asked.

"There're plenty of odd jobs around to keep him busy. Unloading lumber, sweeping, and the like," Papa replied.

Odd jobs. Was that all Papa thought Sammy Joe was good for? "And me?" Fred asked, dreading the answer.

"Same as before—I'll have you rotating in different areas. For now, you'll help repair that hole in the floor." Papa paused a moment. "The *second* floor you've had to repair in less than six months."

Later as they worked together to repair the floor, Alroy asked Fred about the squeal of the whistle.

"It disturbed me that no one was keeping track of the pressure," Fred explained. "So I figured a way to use the whistle as an escape valve if it should overheat. There wasn't enough pressure to blow a clear sound, but I knew from the squeal that it was building dangerously high."

"How long will it take to repair the engine?" one of the men asked.

Fred said, "No repair. Papa's shutting her down for good."

"Nay. I canna believe the man would do such a thing," Alroy said, his face registering his disbelief.

Sammy Joe said, "That old locomotive over at the station is sounding better and better to these old ears."

Fred didn't go straight home after work that evening. He went to Tim's office instead. He had to wait for a few minutes until a client left, then Tim invited him in.

Fred didn't mince any words. "Got room on the floor at your place for me to sleep, Tim? I'm moving out."

"This sounds serious. What happened?"

"Do you call being accused of purposely blowing up my father's factory serious?"

"Very serious indeed. Sit down, Fred. Let's talk."

Once Fred had told the story, Tim agreed it might be best for him to get away for a little while. "Nothing long-term, you understand, just until the air clears," Tim said. "What do you think your mama will say?"

"She's not gonna like it one bit. But I can't live under the same roof with a man who accuses me so unjustly."

Before Fred left, Tim asked, "Do you think Purlee purposely blew up your steam engine?"

Fred thought about the question a moment. He almost wished he could answer yes. If that were so, there might be an investigation. But it just wasn't true.

"Naw," he finally said. "First of all, I don't think he knows enough about the machine to purposely do anything with it. And second, the way he was standing there staring at the thing when it was about to blow is proof certain he was completely daft about the whole thing."

Tim nodded. "Will you be coming over tonight?"

"Just as soon as I throw together a few things. I have a class tonight, but I'll drop my things off before I go."

"I'll leave word with Mrs. Aupperle in the millinery shop that you'll be going in and out so she won't be alarmed."

"Thank you, Tim." Fred reached across the desk to shake his cousin's hand.

"Glad to be of help."

Back at the house, Mama and Julia were scurrying about the kitchen, canning tomatoes from the garden. The entire house held the aroma of stewed tomatoes. Meg was still out working with Dr. Lankford.

With barely a brief nod in their direction, Fred ran upstairs to his room. He took a change of clothes and laid them out on his bed. On top he threw in his comb and brush. With the clothes inside, he rolled up the blankets and cinched his leather belt around the roll. That would be enough to hold him for a while. He wasn't sure what he'd need nor how long he'd be gone. He went to his desk and gathered up his schoolbooks.

When he came through the kitchen with the pack over his

shoulder and arms full of books, Mama just stared at him.

Julia came to his side, wiping her hands on a linen towel. "Fred, what in the world are you doing?"

"I'm leaving for a few days."

Mama gasped and grabbed for a chair to steady herself.

His strong stalwart mama. He didn't think it would affect her so.

"Did you and Papa have another fuss?" Julia wanted to know.

"You can ask him," Fred told her. "He won't listen to me, anyway."

"Where will you go?"

"Cousin Tim's offered to let me room with him."

Mama pulled out the chair she was clinging to and sat down. "Hundreds of people dying of cholera and my son just ups and leaves home."

"I have no choice, Mama. Papa left me no choice." He was ready to go out the door, then stopped and went to give Mama a kiss on her cheek. "I'm sorry. I truly do love you."

At the door, he said to Julia, "Don't forget to lime the privy." And with that he left.

CHAPTER 12
Moving Out

Fred had visited Tim's place over Aupperle's Millinery Shop only one other time, and that had been several months ago. The two rooms were designed to be a bedroom and a sitting room. But just as in his office, Tim had papers, books, and files stacked everywhere.

On the table were two spirit lamps and two coffee pots. Nearby shelves were stocked with coffee, mugs, spoons, and a tin of crackers. Several other tins were there as well, but Fred didn't stop to investigate.

He stowed his bedroll in a corner, placed the stack of books beside it, grabbed the book he needed for class, and hurried on his way.

Night classes during the summer were much more intense

than during the regular school term. Fred hadn't been keeping up with his studies much. He'd been so agitated ever since Mr. Purlee arrived, he could hardly concentrate. Plus, he found he'd rather experiment than read and study. His present class in literature was about the most boring thing he'd ever sat through.

Tim always encouraged Fred to complete his education and get a degree, but now Fred wasn't so sure. Maybe he'd just get a job with the railroad and leave home for good.

The class size was shrinking due to the number of cases of cholera. The very thought of the terrible disease made Fred shudder. How he wished there were some way he could convince Meg to stop going out into the midst of all that sickness.

It was more difficult than ever to listen to the poetry being discussed. Fred simply had too much on his mind to concentrate. As the class drew to a close, he realized he was mighty hungry. His appetite had increased recently and at times seemed almost bigger than he was. He tried to remember what Mama had been preparing—other than tomatoes for canning—when he'd run inside to fetch his things. But he'd been in too big a hurry to notice. If he'd asked, she'd probably have given him something to take with him. But he hadn't.

Well, not to worry, he thought as he hurried down the steps of the lecture hall. After all, Tim wasn't starving. He'd just eat where Tim ate.

When Fred got back to Tim's rooms, his cousin still hadn't come home. Fred wasn't sure where Tim would want him to sleep, so he picked up a book on railroads, lit the gas lamp that hung from the ceiling, and sat down at the table to read and wait. He'd only been reading a short while when he heard steps on the stairs.

Tim came breezing through the door with a smile on his face. "When I saw the light from the street, I was a little surprised. Then I remembered I had a houseguest." He waved his hand about. "Welcome to my humble abode. You can spread your bed out there by the window if you'd like."

For a moment Fred felt a little awkward. When he'd made this plan, it hadn't occurred to him that he might be imposing on his cousin's kindness and breaking into his privacy. He wouldn't like it much if someone came in to share his room at home.

"Have you eaten?" Tim asked.

Fred shook his head.

"I should have thought. I had something earlier, but the hotel just down the street has their table open until late."

"Table?" Fred had never eaten in a hotel in his life.

"All you can eat for a nickel. You have a nickel?"

Fred pulled coins from his pocket and showed Tim.

"Good. It won't be as tasty as your mama's, but it's edible. I'll be right here when you get back. I still have a little work to do before I can turn in."

Eating at the hotel alone seemed a frightening thought, and yet Fred's stomach was complaining loudly. Time to grow up, he chided himself firmly. He grabbed his cap from off the hook by the door. "Be back shortly," he said and headed down the stairs.

Tim was right. Late as it was, there were still men hanging around the hotel lobby. Fred had delivered pamphlets to this lobby before, but he'd never paid any attention to the adjacent dining room. There were small tables set about with snow-white cloths, where people sat chatting and enjoying their meals.

Off to one side was a long table filled with good food.

Fred could see there were cheeses, beef tongue, pink slices of ham, boiled eggs, thick slices of brown bread. The sign by the table said, "All you can eat—five cents." But Fred had no idea who to pay. No one else was taking food from that long table.

Presently, a man approached him. "May I show you to a table, young man?" The man was impeccably dressed in a black suit and starched white shirt with a high stiff collar and black cravat. He was eyeing Fred up and down. Suddenly Fred realized he must look a little down at the heels for such a nice eating place.

"I just stopped in for the nickel dinner," Fred told the man.

"And you have the money." It was both a statement *and* a question.

"Of course." Fred pulled a nickel from his pocket. He resented the tone in the man's voice. "And I'll take the two-cent mug of cider to boot."

"Very well." The man held his upturned palm and Fred paid him. He knew the two cents could have gone to something more important, but he needed to show this man he wasn't broke.

"And where do I go to eat? Any table here?"

"Any table," the man replied, still with that haughty tone.

Tim was right. The food wasn't as tasty as Mama's, but Fred ate his fill and went back for two pieces of apple pie.

As Fred left the hotel to walk back to Tim's house, a large wagon came rattling down the street toward him. It seemed rather strange to see such a large wagon coming down one of the main streets of the city at this late hour. The wagon was nearly beside him before he realized what it was—a "death" wagon carrying bodies of the most recent victims of the cholera epidemic.

Fred stopped and stared as it went lumbering by. Then he bolted and ran the rest of the way to Tim's place, shivering as he went. The death wagons never came through their neighborhood on Everett Street.

When he'd returned to the small rooms above the millinery shop, Tim was in his bedroom with the door closed. Fred's blankets were unrolled and positioned on the floor near the windows that overlooked the street. Tim had added a couple blankets, obviously in an effort to make it softer.

After his heart stopped pounding, Fred pulled off his shoes and socks and plopped down on the blankets. Just then, Tim stuck his head out of his bedroom door. "Get a good supper, Fred?"

"Very good. Thank you. And thanks for letting me know about it."

"Are you going back to work at the factory tomorrow?"

"I'll go back. Unless Papa indicates he doesn't want me there at all."

"I don't think he'd do that."

"We'll see."

"I hope you sleep well. Wish I had better accommodations to offer you."

"No, no. This is just fine. I'm very grateful for all you've done."

After Tim bade him good night, Fred lay restlessly on his makeshift bed. Every time a wagon rumbled down the street, he thought of Meg working among the sick, and he couldn't sleep for worrying about her. Then he thought of Sammy Joe and wondered how much longer he'd stay at the factory doing menial jobs. Then he thought about Papa and wondered if his father cared about him at all. Through it all, the hard floor kept reminding him he wasn't in his soft bed at home. Just before falling asleep, he wondered what he'd eat for breakfast.

The next morning Fred was awakened by Tim shuffling around, preparing to boil coffee over one of the spirit lamps. The pump to fetch water was at the end of the hall. Fred jumped up and offered to go fill the coffee pot.

"Thank you, Fred. I may get used to you real quick. Here, fill this pail while you're at it. You can use that to wash."

At the door, Fred paused. "Is this water from a cistern, Tim?"

"It is. Yes, I know. Henry talked to me as well. I've been very careful about the water I drink."

Fred sighed. "Good." And he went to fetch the water.

When Fred left for work that morning, he had only a few crackers and some coffee on his growling stomach. Tim offered to buy his breakfast, but Fred's pride wouldn't allow him to accept. By midmorning, he wished he'd said yes.

Fred's small wages were usually spent on chemicals and books, but that would have to change. Now he'd have to buy his own food and, if possible, pay Tim something for the rent.

Papa never came downstairs the whole day. Fred and Sammy helped the men repair the floor and set the lathes back into position. Two of the lathes were in need of repair as well. Through it all, Edgar Purlee stood around telling everyone just what to do—in spite of the fact that they already knew what needed to be done.

Fred had told Sammy Joe about moving in with Tim, and Sammy Joe had told the other men. At noon, Alroy noticed that Fred had no lunch. While Mr. Purlee was out of earshot, Alroy spread the word, and all the men shared a little from their lunches. Food had never tasted so good!

"I'm sure gonna miss my mechanized lathe," Alroy said, as he bit into a fat biscuit. "Sure and I never saw a thing make work go so fast. Amazing is what it was. Truly amazing."

"I'll miss the whistle, too," Zeb put in. "How we gonna know when to go to work and when to quit?"

Just then, Edgar walked up. "'Cause I'm gonna tell you when to work and when to quit. And I'm telling you the mid-day break is now over."

Sammy Joe glanced at Fred and rolled his eyes.

Since he had no classes that evening, Fred decided to spend the evening in his laboratory at home. He might not live under Papa's roof, but he felt as though the laboratory was his.

While Fred was busy working, Julia slipped in carrying a plate heaped with ham and baked sweet potatoes, the skins of which were still dark from lying in the ashes of the fireplace. Lying atop the potatoes were slices of Mama's *Hefeküchen*. The day before, pride would have kept Fred from eating the food. But hunger had long since driven his pride away. He thanked Julia and dove into the food.

"Mama saw the lantern light out here, and she told me to bring it."

"Mama did?" Around a mouthful of the salty ham, he said, "Please thank her for me."

"I sure wish you'd come back home, Fred. I miss you already."

"Because you have to lime the privy?" he joked.

"Because you belong with us."

"Papa doesn't seem to think so. He didn't speak to me at all today."

Julia toyed with the magnets on Fred's workbench.

101

"You're both pretty hard-headed," she said. "Meg and I are praying this will be settled quickly. So I'm sure everything will be all right."

"Mama always said you look at the world through rose-colored glasses. I wish you could face reality and see things as they truly are."

Ignoring his remark, she asked, "Are you praying, too, Fred?"

Fred felt ashamed. Mama and Papa both had taught him to seek God and serve God, but he had not. Truth be known, he was angry with God for allowing these terrible things to happen in his life. Turning back to his worktable, Fred said, "That's none of your business, Julia."

"I thought not," she said and closed the door.

Living with Tim had its ups and downs. For one thing, Fred felt hungry most of the time. At home he could go through the kitchen and grab food at any time.

On the other hand, a wonderful advantage was the evenings when he and Tim sat and talked for hours. Tim seemed to enjoy the company, and Fred asked many questions about slavery and the abolitionist movement.

"Tell me, Tim," Fred asked during one such conversation, "what do you think it would take to end slavery forever?"

Solemnly Tim answered, "Many believe—and I agree—it will take nothing less than an all-out war to rid our land of this plague."

Fred had never heard Tim speak such stout words. It was a frightening thought. Almost as frightening as cholera.

By the end of the first week of living with Tim, Fred considered getting a job as a newsboy. He could sell papers early in the mornings before going to the factory. The *Gazette* was right down the street. From his window he could see the boys gathering each morning to get their bundles. Then he heard them calling out the headlines on their various street corners.

Before that plan could be put into action, however, Fred had visitors. Saturday evening, he and Tim were sitting at the table reading when a knock sounded on Tim's door. Tim jumped up to answer it, and Fred heard a deep voice asking for Frederick Allerton. Fred recognized the voice of his uncle Bernhard.

"I'm here, Uncle Bernhard," Fred said, joining Tim at the door. Then he could see Uncle Klassen standing back in the shadow of the hallway.

"Your mama said we'd find you here," said Uncle Bernhard. "May we speak to you a moment?"

Tim stepped back to let them in. "Should I leave?" Tim asked politely.

"Certainly not," said Bernhard, "this will only take a moment."

Mama had three younger sisters, all of whom had married boys from Over-the-Rhine. Good German boys, as Oma called them. And all three families had had only daughters. Fred was the lone grandson on the Schiller side of his family.

Tim was pulling out chairs and clearing books from the table, while Fred lit the spirit lamp to heat the coffee.

"The coffee we do not need now, thank you," said Uncle Bernhard. Turning to Fred, Uncle Bernhard said, "Frederick, we need your help. Cholera is sweeping through German-town like wildfire. We. . ." He pointed to Klassen. "We brothers-in-law think to send Oma Schiller away, keeping her safe from the disease."

"That sounds like a good idea," Tim put in as he joined them at the table. "Where do you plan to send her?"

"A good friend she has in Columbus. Longtime friend, a widow lady named Mrs. Sophie Kirdzik."

"I've heard Oma speak of Sophie many times," Fred said.

Uncle Bernhard nodded then continued. "A month or so ago, Mrs. Kirdzik mails Oma a letter inviting her to come. We believe it is time she should go."

Fred was relieved at this news. "But why are you telling me? What do you want me to do?"

"We will send her on the railroad, but she is terrified. You, her only grandson, will accompany her, yes?"

Fred could hardly believe this blessed turn of events. Finally something good was happening in his life. His first real ride on the railroad. And all the way to Columbus.

CHAPTER 13
Fred's Mission

Fred's uncles explained that they had already talked to Papa and that Papa had given his approval for Fred to go. It was all set. Fred and Oma would leave first thing Monday morning.

The uncles were polite enough not to ask why he was staying at Tim's, and Fred had no idea what Papa and Mama had told them. But that didn't matter. Nothing mattered except that he would be a paying customer on a railroad. It didn't even matter that he would have to go home to pack his things.

After Fred saw his uncles to the door, he turned around to see that Tim was lost in thought.

"What's wrong, Tim? What are you thinking?" Fred sat back down beside his cousin.

"Fred, we have a very important link in the Underground Railroad in Columbus. Brother Coffin and Salmon and I were just yesterday discussing the folks at that stop. Would you consider delivering goods and supplies to them while you're there?"

Excitement welled up inside Fred. "You bet I would," he replied, struggling to keep his voice calm. "Just tell me when and where."

"And *how*. You must be very careful."

"I'll be careful." At long last, he'd be doing more than delivering pamphlets. Just what he'd been hoping for.

"Say nothing to any of your family members."

That wouldn't be too hard. "I won't say a word to anyone."

"We'll have the supplies shipped on the baggage car. You rent a livery to take your Oma to her friend's, then return to the station and pick up the parcels. We'll also supply you with money to purchase staples at the grocery. If anyone asks, you just tell them you're visiting relatives and you wanted to bless them with supplies. Think you can do all that?"

"I can do that just fine."

Before the trip, Fred met with Salmon Chase and Levi Coffin in the back room of Brother Coffin's store for further directions. He was given a map of directions from the town out to the farm of Mr. and Mrs. Tibbets. After having his abilities doubted by Papa for so long, it felt good to be trusted by these men and by his uncles as well. Before Fred left the store, Brother Coffin offered up a solemn prayer for Fred's wisdom and safety.

Both the Purlee sisters were at the Allertons' when Fred went home Sunday afternoon to pack. Seeing them there grated on his nerves and reminded him afresh of the problems he'd had with their father. How he wished Julia had never met Etta in the first place.

As usual they were sitting on the front porch, busy with their handwork. Mama was with them. As Fred stopped to give Mama a kiss on the cheek, Julia said, "I wish I were a boy. Then maybe I would be chosen to accompany Oma instead of you."

"But you're not," Fred replied and went on inside the house.

After packing a few clothes into the family's one valise, he slipped out through the kitchen to his laboratory. In among his clothes he packed his two batteries. They might come in handy.

When he came back out to the front porch, Mama said to him, "We miss you, Frederick."

"I know, Mama. I miss you, too. But some things just can't be helped."

He happened to glance over at Molly, who was gazing at him, her pretty eyes clear and wide. Those eyes made him most uncomfortable. He glared back at her. Why couldn't the two sisters just stay at their own house with their own hateful, pro-slavery papa? Why'd they have to come here anyway?

Mama was getting up. "I have a few things for you," she said. He followed her inside so he wouldn't have to stand there waiting as Molly Purlee stared at him.

Mama had fixed a package of bread, pork, cheese, and boiled eggs. "For your supper," she said. "Another I will bring when we come to the station in the morning."

"You're coming to see me off?"

"But of course we come. The girls and I, we come."

"Thank you, Mama." He kissed her cheek again and hurried out before she made him cry.

When Mama had said "the girls and I," Fred had no idea she

meant the Purlee girls as well. But there they were, along with Meg and Julia, bright and early Monday morning at the CH&D railroad station.

The nerve of some people. He pulled Meg aside. "What are *they* doing here?" he asked, fairly spitting the words.

"The four of us are spending a good deal of time together these days."

"So I've noticed."

"I don't know how you could, since you don't live with us anymore."

Fred let the sharp words pass over him, reminding himself that moving out had been his idea. "What are they doing here at the station?" he asked again.

"Julia and I invited them," Meg answered quietly. "It's as simple as that."

Looking down toward the other end of the station platform, he caught a glimpse of Sister Catharine Coffin, her gray dress sweeping the wooden platform as she walked. She caught his eye and nodded. That meant the supplies were safely loaded.

Just then the carriage arrived, bringing Mama's three sisters, several of the girl cousins, and Oma. Amid a flood of tears and way too many hugs, they finally got aboard. Oma, dressed in her black silk widow's dress, fairly clung to Fred as they went up the stairs onto the coach. Fred could tell she was frightened. It was difficult to think about Oma's fear when he was so excited.

"You want to sit by the window, Oma?" he asked politely.

"Only until we begin moving—so I can wave good-bye to my precious ones." She sat down and lifted the wispy veil of her black bonnet. Suddenly the shrill whistle gave off a loud blast, and Oma grabbed for Fred's arm.

"It's all right, Oma." He patted her hand. "The noise won't hurt you. It's just the whistle." He helped her to sit down, putting her bag at her feet. True to her word, Mama had given Fred a package with his lunch packed inside. He put it down beside his valise.

Once they were seated and Oma had waved to all her daughters and granddaughters for the hundredth time, the train whistle sounded, the conductor called out the "all aboard," and the train lurched with the grating sound of metal scraping against metal. Fred thought Oma was going to faint, and he wasn't sure what he'd do if she did.

It took several miles before she was able to settle down and relax. Fred was now by the window, watching with interest as the scenery flew past. It was a relief to get away from all the problems of Cincinnati, especially the horrid pall of the threat of cholera. When the conductor came to collect the tickets, Fred asked if he could go up front to see the locomotive.

"You would not leave me here?" Oma said nervously.

"You'll be fine, Oma. I just want to see the engine while it's in operation." Then he told the conductor about the steam engine he'd built and how it ran the lathes in his papa's factory. He didn't mention that it *used* to run the lathes in his papa's factory.

"Why it'd pleasure old Ike to no end to have you come take a look," he said kindly. "And, ma'am," he said to Oma. "You'll be just fine. Why look here." He pointed a row over and back one seat. "Here's a fine lady who'll sit with you for a few moments."

The other lady, who looked to be near Oma's age, appeared as though she rode the coaches every day. Somehow the sight of her had a calming effect on Oma. That was

all Fred needed. He was out of his seat, following the conductor to the front of the train. He had to crawl up a ladder
and shinny across a plank over the tender car loaded with
black coal, an exciting challenge.

The engineer named Ike gave Fred a full explanation of
how the train operated, down to the last little gauge and the
brakes. Fred watched as the fireman shoveled in the coal just
as fast as he could. Sammy Joe would be great at that job.

Fred loved the feel of the wind in his face, the sound of
the whistle, the hissing of the steam spigots, and the burning
of coal smoke in his nose. Perhaps he would seek out a job
on the railroad after all. What fun this would be—the thrill
of moving along at thirty-five miles an hour. Why, they'd be
in Columbus before suppertime. It was a pure miracle.

Soon after Fred was sitting with Oma once again, they
took out their lunches. Oma was sure she couldn't eat a bite
traveling along at such a speed. "Curdle in my stomach, it
will," she declared. But in the end, she did eat. And she held
it all just fine.

When the train stopped for water at Xenia, they were
more than halfway to Columbus. In no time at all, the conductor was announcing the approach to the large town.
Suddenly Fred grew somewhat nervous. The gravity of the
job he'd been assigned suddenly hit him. He alone would be
responsible for getting the supplies to the folks at this important station of the Underground Railroad.

After he assisted Oma down from the train coach at
Columbus, he took her inside the station and guided her to a
bench. He instructed her to wait for him while he walked to
the nearby livery to rent the wagon and team. She seemed to
be a little weary, but more peaceful now. The frightening part
was over.

The livery had a good matched team of sorrels—gentle and easy to handle. Tim had told him it might cost about twenty dollars, and he was right on the money. The wagon was a sturdy buckboard with high sides. Just what Fred would need for transporting the supplies.

Oma had the address of Sophie Kirdzik, and the station master gave Fred directions. After loading their small valises and Oma's trunk, Fred drove her to the house, three blocks from the main street of town. Sophie had been watching for them and came scurrying down the front walk as they pulled up.

Fred hitched the team and assisted Oma down to the ground, after which the two friends embraced and shed a few tears. They began talking in their native German, only a few phrases of which Fred could catch. He heaved Oma's trunk down from the back of the wagon.

"Where shall I take this?" he asked.

The ladies noticed him then, and Oma introduced him to Sophie. Sophie had been on the ship with Oma and Opa when they'd come to America. They'd known one another that long. Fred could hardly fathom that many years.

Once Oma's things were taken inside and she was settled, Sophie insisted he join them for tea. But Fred politely refused. "I have an errand to run for my cousin Tim," he told them.

"You will be here for the night?" asked Sophie. "The guest room is ready."

"I'm not sure," he said. And he wasn't. He knew his delivery would take him a ways out of town, but he didn't know exactly how far. "Don't wait up for me." Turning to kiss his Oma, he told her, "If I'm not back this evening, I'll be sure to come and say good-bye to you before I leave to go home tomorrow."

"See that you do," she replied.

Almost before he was out the door, the two were again chattering on in German.

Fred drove the wagon back to the station, and with the help of a young black station worker, he loaded the supplies that had been sent by the Cincinnati abolitionist group. As they loaded on the last crate, the young man leaned over closer to Fred and said, "Those men over there be your friends?"

Fred glanced over to the corner of the station to see two men on horseback sitting easy in the saddle. "No friends of mine."

"They sure be keeping an eagle eye on you."

Fred could feel their eyes. Tim had often described slave catchers to Fred. "They're nothing more than glorified bounty hunters," Tim would say. "They're in the saddle most of the time, and they look weathered and worn." The two men fit that description exactly.

Fred felt a funny tightness in his midsection. He remembered something else Tim had said: "A stranger in a town the size of Columbus will be suspect. Keep your eyes open."

CHAPTER 14
Making the Delivery

When Fred asked the station worker for directions to the mercantile, he replied, "Second block on Main, hard by the shoemaker's place."

"Thank you," Fred told him. He fished in his pocket for a coin, paid him, then surprised the man by shaking his hand. "I appreciate your help."

The man's eyes lit up. "I'm sure glad to do it. Watch your step now."

At the mercantile, Fred purchased the items on the list written in Brother Coffin's hand. Flour, cornmeal, sugar, coffee, salt, crackers—good basic staples needed for feeding many hungry mouths. As the man was tabulating the ticket, Fred asked, "Got any wire?"

"Got all kinds of wire." The man looked at him over a pair of small, round eyeglasses. "Just what kind would you like?"

"Stovepipe wire will do just fine."

"Over here."

Fred followed him to where the hardware items were located.

"How much you need?"

Fred did some quick calculating. "About forty feet."

"Forty feet it is." The proprietor measured the wire and cut it with wire cutters, coiled the wire, and placed it on top of the other supplies.

"Throw in a few fence staples as well," Fred said, adding, "Mind if I bring the wagon around back to load this?"

"Be easier for me if you did," the man said, handing Fred the ticket.

Fred took a bill from his pocket and paid for the supplies, stuffing the change in a pocket. The other money he'd been given he'd slipped into his brogans that morning. The stout, heavy shoes made a good hiding place.

As he went out on the front steps, he looked down the street to see the two men leaning against the bank building at the corner. Their horses were hitched at the rail out front. He still couldn't be sure they were watching him.

Driving the wagon into the alley, Fred and the proprietor made quick work of loading. Then Fred took just a moment to string the wire around the edge of the buckboard.

The proprietor had gone back inside. No one seemed to be watching. Just as well. There was more than enough wire to wind it around twice, keeping it close to the top edge and fastening it here and there with the fence staples. A rock served as a makeshift hammer.

Before pulling out, Fred put the change from the purchase in his shoes with the rest of his cash, took out the map Salmon Chase had drawn, and memorized it. The Tibbetses' farm was several miles out of town, but Fred figured he'd still be there before dark.

Outside Columbus, fertile farmland stretched out on either side of the road. As the wagon rattled along, a summer's worth of dust billowed up and coated Fred from head to toe. The map showed a creek a ways up the road. He'd stop there and get a drink.

Fred didn't know exactly how he knew he was being followed. He just knew. When he was asked to make this delivery to help the cause, he never imagined he'd be afraid. But a very real fear was welling up on his insides, and he could taste it in his mouth—all brassy and sharp.

Were they thieves? Would they rob him? Were they slave catchers who suspected his mission? His valise was at his feet. Still holding the reins loosely, he reached down and pulled out a battery. Next he grabbed one end of the stovepipe wire and fastened it securely to the pin on top of the battery. His rigging was probably a futile effort. If the men wanted anything, they could just shoot him and be done with it.

For years, Fred had listened to the stories of the heroic efforts of those of the abolition movement. Why even Mr. Chase had been pelted with eggs and attacked by mobs. But Fred didn't feel one bit heroic, just terribly frightened. He was a stranger in a strange place. Totally alone. Except for God. But he hadn't talked to God for ever so long. Fred wasn't even sure they were on speaking terms.

The ruby sun touched the horizon as he moved from the

farmlands into a wooded area. The little remaining sunlight was dimmed by the thick stands of trees. Presently, he came to the creek. The water was about three feet deep at the ford. Thirsty as he was, it seemed too big a chance to stop and get out. He kept a gloved hand on the battery and the free end of the wire.

"Stop that wagon right there, kid!" a voice called out. In front of him, two men stepped out from the trees onto the roadway—the same two men he'd seen in town. They were on foot. They must have ridden on ahead of him, left the horses in the brush, and snuck up to the road on foot. One was tall and skinny and as bow-legged as Fred had ever seen a man. The other was all muscle and sinew, built like a bear.

Fred pulled on the reins. Under his breath, he was praying. Praying hard.

"Say there, young'n," called the bear. "Where you goin' with all that stuff you got in that there wagon?"

"I'm God's delivery boy," Fred heard himself say.

Both men threw back their heads and hooted with laughter. "Whooee!" the tall one whooped. "Don't that beat all you ever did hear, Ned? We done heared it all now. This here's God's delivery boy."

Both men carried Hawken rifles. The bear had his cradled loosely in his arms. But the tall man's was cocked and primed.

"Tell me," said the bear, "just what does God's delivery boy carry?"

"Sometimes I have ordinary stuff," Fred told them. "But today I have a load of lightning. Come and look."

The men looked at one another and again burst into loud guffaws. "The boy's daft," said the skinny man.

Fred's remark seemed to have taken them off guard. They both waded into the creek. "Keep him covered, Billy," said the bear. "I'm gonna have a look at this here lightning he's talking about." The man came up to the wagon and grabbed onto the edge to peer in.

Billy's rifle was aimed straight at Fred's midsection. With the least bit of movement, Fred touched the free end of the wire to the battery with his gloved hand. As the electricity charged through the two strands of wire, a caterwauling went up like Fred had never heard before, something akin to the cry of a wounded bobcat.

"Help!" Ned hollered, dropping his rifle in the creek. "Help me, Billy. This thing won't turn me loose."

Fred knew the water was acting as a conductor of the electricity and that the man was getting more than just a little buzz. Billy sloshed through the water to grab his friend, but when he locked onto him, the electricity shot through both men. The second rifle splashed into the creek, and the men screamed for all they were worth.

"God's lightning is all powerful!" Fred called out. In the same movement, he released the wire from the battery and gave the reins a hard shake. With a loud shout, he let the team take their head. They flew up out of that creek bed, spraying water everywhere. As he looked back, he saw both men on their backsides, floundering about in the water.

By the time he was through the woods, Fred found he was trembling like a leaf in a gale force wind. Never had he been so scared. Over and over, he kept saying, "I'm sorry, Lord. I'm so sorry. Please forgive me. I didn't know how much I needed You till now."

Two miles past the creek in a shallow valley lay the Tibbetses' farm—a welcome sight. The trim, two-story farmhouse was flanked by a large barn, a number of sheds, and a granary. At the farmhouse he was greeted with warm hospitality. Noah and Minerva Tibbets were kind, gentle folk who were unspeakably grateful for all the fresh supplies. They unloaded at the back door of the house, then took the wagon to the barn just in case he'd been followed. But Fred didn't think he'd have any more trouble with those two men.

He showed his rigging to the Tibbetses, and they joined in laughing with him over the incident. He let them touch the live wire and feel the buzzing sensation, then explained how the water made it even stronger.

"Guess the good Lord knows all about water and that there electricity," quipped Noah, a weathered farmer with a full black beard. "Yes, sir. He surely does."

Fred asked if they thought the men were slave catchers.

Noah shrugged. "Don't matter," he said. "Men who come at you with loaded rifles don't aim to do you any good." He started unhitching the team. "You're staying the night, ain't you?"

"Why of course he's staying the night." Minerva patted Fred's shoulder. "Now you come along, son, and we'll fix you something to eat. Mr. Tibbets will take care of the team just fine."

The Tibbetses' large open kitchen was filled with the aroma of beans. Fred saw the full kettle hanging on a hook in the fireplace. Juicy ham hocks floated about in the bubbling pot, with little spots of grease shining on top.

He watched as Minerva ladled out a large bowl and put steaming yellow cornbread on a side plate. Hungry as he was, Fred took a moment to bow his head and return thanks. He didn't believe he'd ever forget again.

While Fred ate, Minerva sorted through the crate of clothing he had delivered, admiring each item.

"Tell me, Mrs. Tibbets," Fred said when he'd finished off about half the food. "Why do you do this dangerous work? I know of people who have been taken to court and lost fortunes for helping runaways. Some have had their houses burned down."

Minerva Tibbets looked at him. She had a round, cheerful face with laughing eyes. "Fred," she said, "have you ever seen a group of runaway slaves?"

Fred shook his head. He knew they came to the basement of Levi Coffin's store by the scores and into the attics of many homes in Cincinnati, but he'd not seen them.

"They're so frightened, so weary, so hungry. Footsore and half naked. Some wounded and some ill. And yet undaunted. Their courage is a wonderful thing to behold."

A faraway look came into the eyes of this common farmer's wife. "Once you've seen the courage and determination, the smiles of gratitude, you can never turn them away. I'd lay down my very life to help them. And Noah feels the same way I do."

"Aren't you ever frightened?"

"Most of the time," she confessed. "But we pray, and God helps us through it. Our lives are in His hands."

As she spoke, she reached again into the crate and lifted out a pink crocheted layette. "Oh my," she said. "Would you just look at this? I've never seen anything so purty in all my born days." She fingered the ruffled edges. "Much love went into this work," she said. "I know of very few women who can master this special ruffle stitch."

Fred paid polite attention as she pointed out the intricacies of the pattern, but his mind was thinking about what she had said earlier about their lives being in God's hands. As he bedded down in their upstairs spare bedroom that night, Fred could see how he'd been taking his life out of God's hands and trying to run everything himself. He was suddenly ashamed of all his angry words. Could he do better? He wasn't sure. All he could do was to pray for God to help him.

CHAPTER 15

Back Home

The next day, when Fred returned to Columbus, Oma asked him to stay over another day. It seemed her friend Sophie needed a number of repairs done around the house, and Oma had volunteered Fred for the job. Fred didn't mind at all. Another day away from Cincinnati suited him just fine.

As luck would have it, the same engineer was manning the controls in the locomotive on Fred's return trip the next day. Ike let him ride in the locomotive the entire way from Columbus to Cincinnati!

Fred had only been away for three days, but it seemed much longer. As he reported on his trip at the abolitionists' meeting, he felt older somehow. He was commended for a job well done, but he felt none of the pride he thought he'd feel. Compared to people like Minerva Tibbets, his delivery was nothing. Nothing at all.

Work at the factory was more difficult than ever. Fred couldn't abide looking at Edgar Purlee. Yes, Fred had called on God when he needed Him desperately, but he couldn't stop hating this pig-eyed man who'd caused so much destruction. To make matters worse, he learned about Sammy Joe. His friend was gone.

"Said he couldn't take it no longer," Alroy told Fred. "Old Purlee seemed to think he could crack down on Sammy Joe if you weren't here to protect him."

"We told him to stay around till you came back," Zeb added, "but he didn't even finish out the day. Said he'd pick up his pay later on and he was gone."

Fred felt empty. He and Sammy Joe had spent every day side by side for two years. Now he was gone. And all because of Edgar Purlee.

"What did Papa say?"

"Don't know as he said nothing," Zeb remarked.

How could that be? Fred couldn't understand it. Several men were out from the cholera, and with the steam-driven lathes at a standstill, production at the factory was at a low ebb. If Fred were running the factory, he wouldn't hire any pro-slavery men, he'd have steam power for every lathe, and he'd keep close tabs on every employee. What good was it to turn out quality products if the entire place wasn't managed well?

The cholera epidemic was changing a number of things. Fred learned that Tim was rethinking his plans for marriage.

"Hearing those wagons rumbling through the streets has made me think differently about Dot and me getting married,"

Tim explained to Fred. "We've moved the date from December to the first of September."

Fred knew that meant he'd have to find another place to live. An unannounced visit from Mama a few days later settled that issue for good. His mama seldom came into town. She spent more time shopping Over-the-Rhine than in downtown Cincinnati. But there she was, standing at the door dressed in her plain straw bonnet and tan shawl. She dressed almost as simply as Catharine Coffin.

It was early evening and only by luck had she caught him there. Or was it the Lord? Fred had begun to think much more about the Lord's presence in his life. He politely invited her to come in and sit down.

"I would be pleased to have you come home," she said to him. "People every day dying off, sometimes in just a few hours. What tomorrow will bring, we do not know. It is best we be together as family for now."

How could he say no?

Being on his own had been good, and he wasn't sorry he'd left. If nothing else, he certainly appreciated his mama's cooking more. But more than that, he'd learned more about making his own decisions and how to handle the little bit of money that he had.

He invited Mama inside and fixed her a cup of coffee. Fortunately, there was a loaf of rye bread on the cabinet shelf, so he was able to fix her a slice of bread and butter. It felt strange to be serving his own mama.

Though he agreed to return home, Fred decided not to do so that very evening. Or even the next day. He waited till the end of the week. He wasn't trying to be belligerent. The extra days gave him time to think things out.

He was going to miss being around Tim, miss their late

night talks. Fred wished he were more like his cousin. When he said that to Tim on their last evening together, Tim replied, "Time takes care of a number of things in our lives, Fred. You're still young. What you see in me that you admire has come mostly through age and experience. Set your heart to do God's will, and you'll become exactly what He wants you to be."

Then Tim surprised Fred by saying a prayer for him. It wasn't a long prayer, but a nice one.

It took awhile for Fred to get used to his own bed again. Now that his body was used to a hard floor, the bed felt all mushy.

The other change he noticed wasn't as simple to fix. Julia had become quiet and pensive. When he tried to joke and laugh with her, there was little or no response. Taking Meg aside, Fred asked what had happened to his little sister.

"It's all the deaths," Meg said softly. "Several of her friends at school have died. She's grieving. We're all grieving. It's a sad time, Fred."

"So many times I've said I wished she'd have to face reality. I should never have wished such a thing, let alone said it."

"Fred, sooner or later we all face reality, no matter what anyone says or does. You have, and I have."

Fred hadn't thought of it that way. What Meg said was true. Both of them had faced much in the past few months.

"I'm grateful to have you home again." She touched his arm. "We're all so thankful that Oma is safe. You were brave to take her."

"It wasn't bravery, Meg. I selfishly wanted to ride the railroad. I was thinking more about me than her." It was a painful confession. He wasn't even sure why he made it.

Meg smiled her gentle smile. "You did it. That's all that matters."

Fred worked in the accounting offices the week following his return to live at home. The books told the story of the sharp downturn in production. He could see the looks of concern on the men who worked daily with the invoices and statements. The number of finished pieces being loaded on the boats at the landing was way down. Was Papa going to let things go on this way indefinitely?

"Have you shown these figures to Papa?" Fred demanded in a conversation with Jesse, the head accountant.

"Now that's a strange question," Jesse replied.

Fred was immediately sorry for his harsh tone. He was sounding like Edgar Purlee. "I'm sorry, Jesse. It's just that I'm surprised Papa knows of the situation yet does nothing about it."

"So am I," Jesse said. "So am I."

"Prepare a statement for me showing the difference between production before the steam engine blew and after. Would you do that?"

Jesse shook his head. "It'll only get me into trouble. You want the figures, do it yourself."

"Will you at least check them for me?"

"That I'll do."

By late afternoon, Fred had the needed papers in hand, and he went boldly into Papa's office, demanding that Papa look at them.

Papa studied them then laid them down on the desk. "These things are only temporary, Frederick. All businesses face downturns now and again. We're prepared to weather the storm."

"But we don't need to weather the storm. I'll repair the boiler and with the steam engine running again, the production will increase. Even without the men you've lost, we can regain some of the lost production."

"I don't want to talk about that steam engine. I've had nightmares about the damage it could have done. We were just lucky that time."

"We *weren't* just lucky." Fred was on his feet now, fuming mad. "I rigged that whistle to warn us if the pressure was too high because I didn't trust that lamebrained Mr. Edgar Purlee. He—"

"Frederick Allerton, bridle your tongue! You'll not speak of my employees in that manner."

Fred took a breath and clenched his fist. "Papa, we're coming into a new age. An age of machines and increased mechanization. You must be ready for it or you'll miss out."

"Then I'll miss out," Papa replied with a sigh. "You may go now."

That evening after work, Fred walked to the railroad with the intent of asking if they needed an extra hand. He was on the threshold of the station ready to go in and talk to the station master when he remembered Mama's words: "What tomorrow will bring, we do not know. It is best we be together as family for now."

For now. Just for now. Fred would put up with it for now. But as soon as the epidemic was over, he would leave. Leave home, leave the factory, perhaps even leave Cincinnati.

If the day had not gone badly enough, when he arrived home, he was met by Etta and Molly. This time, they were not on the front porch but were in the Allerton kitchen. They were busy making a pot of soup. "To take to families who have sick ones," Julia explained when Fred arrived.

He was in no mood for chit chat. Fred couldn't stand to think of the Purlees just now, let alone have two Purlees right in his own kitchen. How he wished he were still at Tim's.

He headed straight for the back door. He'd spend the evening in his laboratory.

"And where do you think you are going, young man?" Mama demanded. "Where are your manners? Kindly greet our guests."

"Hello, Fred," Etta said, stepping closer to Julia as though for protection.

"Afternoon, Fred," Molly echoed as she turned from stirring the kettle of soup—the aroma of which set Fred's mouth to watering.

"Hello," he replied curtly and went out the door. In his laboratory he sat down in his cane-bottomed chair, tipped it back against the wall, folded his arms, and got quiet. He felt terrible. When would he ever be able to stop hating?

After the Purlee sisters had left, Julia came out to tell Fred supper was ready. "I'd have telegraphed you," she said, "but I've been too busy to memorize the Morse code."

"Busy helping Meg?"

"Some. I can't be around the sick people like she is, but I can help with food." Julia was quiet for a moment. "I wish I could have gone to Columbus with you."

Fred suddenly felt selfish for having time away. "I wish you could have, too," he said. "Truly I do."

"Lately, I've wished I could just hop on a train or a steamboat and run away. Sometimes I wish I'd gone with the Hendrickses."

Fred could hardly believe his ears. Was this truly Julia talking, echoing the very things he'd been feeling? "What do you do when you feel that way?" he asked her.

She picked up Fred's Bible lying on the workbench. Since he'd come back from Columbus, he'd brought it out to the laboratory and put it with his other books. "I read this," she said. She thumbed through the pages, turning to the book of Psalms. "Listen to what King David has to say, Fred: 'And I said, Oh that I had wings like a dove! for then would I fly away, and be at rest. . .I would hasten my escape from the windy storm and tempest.'"

Fred was amazed. The mighty King David felt the same way—he, too, wanted to run away and escape.

"When I read this," Julia said softly, "it's like God is saying to me that it's all right to feel that way sometimes. I can't explain it exactly, but it makes me feel better."

Fred studied Julia's face. She seemed to have grown up before his very eyes.

"Come on," she said, returning the Bible to its place. "Mama's waiting supper on us."

Fred didn't really want to go in to supper. He didn't want to look at Papa. But he knew he couldn't avoid the family forever, so he got up and followed Julia into the house.

As they ate, Meg talked of the things she'd learned while treating the sick and how a number of patients were now surviving with correct treatment. "If we can just get to them on time," she added.

Looking directly at Fred, she added, "Molly has become a dedicated worker, and Dr. Lankford sings her praises. He feels she'll make an excellent nurse one day."

Fred looked away. He supposed pro-slavery people could make good nurses and doctors and whatever else they needed to be. But they were still just that—pro-slavery! Southern sympathizers.

Later that evening, Fred was walking through the front hallway toward the stairs when a new doily on the hall table caught his attention. He stepped closer to look. Just as he thought. It was the same intricate ruffled stitch that Mrs. Tibbets had admired in the baby dress. He moved aside the lamp with the roses painted on the glass chimney, picked up the doily, and studied it more closely.

So. It had been his own sisters who were making things for the Underground Railroad. What a surprise.

"You like it?" Meg had walked up behind him with fat Goldie in her arms.

"Very nice. You do this?"

She shook her head. "I've worked and worked to perfect that stitch, but I'm just not that good. The only person I know who does it perfectly is Molly Purlee. That doily is a gift from her to our family."

Fred couldn't believe it. "Her mother does the stitch as well, I suppose?" he asked.

"Molly learned it from some lady in Pittsburgh. Her mama prefers knitting and embroidery over crochet."

Carefully, Fred replaced the doily and put the lamp back on it.

"Fred, is anything wrong? You've acted so strangely since you've come back."

"Nothing's wrong, Meg. Nothing." And with that he ran outside to his laboratory and shut himself in.

Could he have been wrong about Molly? He'd been so sure of himself. How could he have been so wrong?

CHAPTER 16
Setting the Record Straight

The next day, Mr. Purlee was not at the factory. Fred was relieved. The man's absence gave him the perfect opportunity to go to the basement and give the steam engine a thorough going over. It sickened him to see it sitting idle. All his work was wasted.

Inch by inch he went over every working part. Then he found it. Why hadn't he thought of it before? The safety valve. All along he'd wondered why the valve hadn't blown out and prevented the explosion. Now he could see why. Because Purlee was negligent about cleaning the boiler periodically, the valve was coated with sediment. When the boiler overheated, the sediment protected the valve from the heat so the valve didn't melt.

At least now he knew for sure. If he'd been taking care of the engine, it never would have blown.

When he returned upstairs, Alroy told him the news: Edgar Purlee had cholera.

Just prior to the midday break, Fred saw Mama, Meg, and Julia come in the door of the factory. He could hardly believe his eyes. The three of them seldom, if ever, visited the factory. There was no need—except in an emergency. Could something be wrong?

Fred dropped what he was doing and rushed to them. Meg and Julia were both red-eyed, and Julia was dabbing at her face with her hankie. They'd walked a long way in the August heat—from their home all the way to the landing.

"What's wrong?" Fred asked. "What is it?"

Julia burst into tears and couldn't talk.

"It's Etta." Meg pressed her hand to her lips to stop a sob.

"Cholera?" Fred asked.

"Horrible disease," Mama said. "Does not care who it takes."

"Not little Etta?" She was just a little girl. Surely she couldn't have died. "Want me to rent a livery? I'll take you all home," Fred said. He couldn't let them go back out into the heat in their condition.

"Edgar Purlee is ill as well," Mama explained. "He is asking for Benjamin. We must all go there. As a family."

Fred turned to Alroy, who was staring at this strange intrusion into the workday. "Alroy," Fred said, "please go up to Papa's office and tell him to come. I'm going over to the livery."

Without asking Papa, Fred rented a covered buggy that

would seat all five of them comfortably. If Papa didn't like it, he could just take it from Fred's pay. But Papa said nothing. He even allowed Fred to drive the team. Mama asked Fred to stop by the house first so she could fetch food to take to the family.

When they finally arrived at the Purlee home, Fred was shocked. While the house wasn't as rundown as the shanties around the landing, it wasn't a very nice place. There was a look of neglect about it, rather like the steam engine after Purlee took charge, Fred thought. Then he chided himself for thinking ill of a man who might be on his deathbed.

Dr. Lankford's buggy was parked out front. Fred was certainly glad. He knew Henry wouldn't let any of them take undue chances with the contagious disease.

Mrs. Purlee had yet two smaller daughters at home, and Fred could tell the woman was at her wit's end. As they entered the front room, Meg and Mama went right to Mrs. Purlee and commenced to comfort her, while Julia dried her eyes and gathered the little ones, who looked to be about two and four, up in her arms. Fred was amazed at the tenderness displayed by both his sisters.

Dr. Lankford stepped into the hallway and called to Papa. "Benjamin, please come. He's asking for you."

Fred watched as Papa strode down the hallway toward the back bedroom. Just then Molly came into the room, greeting all of them with a weak smile.

"Fred," Mama said, "please to the buggy you go to bring the food we brought."

Fred looked at Molly. "I could use an extra pair of hands," he said softly.

She nodded and went out before him as he held the door.

He stopped at the rickety porch steps, which sorely needed

repair. "I. . .I'm so sorry about little Etta."

"We've learned so much," she said quietly. "I've worked right beside Dr. Lankford. I've seen people live through it. So why. . .?" Her voice broke into a sob. "I thought sure we could save her. My own little sister."

Fred felt horribly awkward. Words caught in his throat. Less than a week ago, he would have had much to say to Molly Purlee. Now no words would come.

Looking up at him with tear-filled eyes, Molly said, "I'm sorry. I've been trying to be strong for Mama and the little ones—"

"Please," Fred interrupted her. "Please don't apologize. No reason to. I just. . .well. . ." His silly stammering embarrassed him.

"You didn't need help with the food, did you?" she asked gently.

"No. I just wanted to ask you. Have you been making clothes for the Underground Railroad?"

Molly's wet eyes grew wide. "How could you possibly know that?"

"Does your papa know?"

She shook her head. "He'd disown me. Us. Mama and I both. And Etta. I mean, Etta used to help. Etta's the one who talked us into it. She kept saying it was the least we could do. Papa thinks it's for a sewing circle that donates to charity."

"And it is. I mean, in a way it is."

"It's a difficult tightrope we walk since Papa has sold out to the pro-slavery movement. But how did you know?"

Fred told her about the journey he'd made to Columbus and how Minerva Tibbets had admired Molly's crochet work. "So when I saw the doily on our hall table with the same stitch. . ."

Molly's eyes lit up. "You actually made a delivery for the Underground Railroad?" Admiration shone in her eyes. "I've marveled at your courage to go to the abolitionist meetings when your father doesn't even agree with you. I've told Julia and Meg so many times that I wished I could be as brave as you. You're a fine man, Frederick Allerton."

"You told them that?"

She nodded.

Fred felt himself withering into a tiny heap of nothing. His sisters knew all along and didn't say a word. How could they have gone on letting him think the worst about this girl?

"My papa makes me very angry at times," Molly went on, "and hurts my feelings often. But I must forgive him. I pray for God to give me grace to love him."

"But all along I thought that you. . ."

She reached out and touched his arm. "I know. But it doesn't matter now, does it? I would have thought the same about you had the circumstances been reversed."

She was being gracious. Fred didn't deserve a smidgen of her graciousness. And he knew it.

"I am very sorry," he said.

She smiled. "And I accept your apology. That was simple, wasn't it? Now what are we carrying in?"

As they were walking in the front door, Papa appeared. "Fred. Mr. Purlee would like a few words with you."

Fred's face must have gone pale because Papa said, "It's all right. Henry says you'll be fine." Papa's eyes were red.

"The man is dying, Fred," Papa went on. "He's already admitted to me that he'd never been in charge of a steam engine in his life. Worked on one, but never been in charge. When a man faces death, truth suddenly becomes very important, and remorse becomes pure agony."

Fred swallowed over the lump in his throat. Mutely he followed Papa down the hall into a small bedroom. The stench of sickness and impending death were overwhelming. Fred wasn't sure he could stand there. He wanted to run. But the presence of his older sister, Meg, helping Dr. Lankford steadied Fred.

He looked at the bed piled with quilts. Edgar Purlee lay shivering. His beefy face had a blue tinge to it.

"Frederick." Edgar's voice was weak and raspy. "I done already made it right with God and your papa. Now I gotta make it right with you." He stopped and coughed. Dr. Lankford stepped forward and gave him a sip of water.

Fred wondered if he were supposed to say something. Or if he was simply going to faint dead away on the floor. Just then, he felt Papa's hand strong and firm on his shoulder.

"Them papers was phony. I ain't never took care of no steam engine. They fixed papers so's I could get a good job. They needed me here. They said abolitionists destroy the economy. Ruin the nation. Gotta get 'em, they told me. Gotta get 'em."

The man closed his eyes and Fred could see the tears seep from the corners of his eyes and roll slowly down through his frowsy beard and into his ears.

How could Fred have ever felt threatened by this man? All the hate he'd ever felt just melted away.

"You saved my life," the raspy voice went on. "You had no call to. I'd a been scalded bad if you and that black boy, that Sammy Joe fella—" Coughing again. Worse this time. "I told your papa you're a fine son. Fine son. Shoulda—he shoulda listened to you."

The hand on Fred's shoulder tightened.

Suddenly Fred said, "Have you talked to Molly?"

134

Edgar forced a weak smile. "I aim to do that. Too late for little Etta. I trust she knows." The coughing came again, the worst yet, and Dr. Lankford ushered them all out.

Later, Henry told them Edgar wouldn't make it until morning. Meg chose to stay and be with Molly and her family through the night. As the Allertons departed, Julia promised to come back to help Mrs. Purlee with the little ones.

Fred unhitched the team and climbed back into the buggy. He turned to see Molly waving to him from the front window. Suddenly it dawned on him that Molly had called him a man. He was a year younger than she, yet she'd called him a man. Something inside his chest swelled a bit.

Beside him, Julia was weeping for the loss of her dear friend. Fred reached over and put a comforting arm around her shoulder—something he'd never done before. "You were a good friend to Etta," he said to her. "She couldn't have had a better friend. I'm proud you're my sister."

Julia smiled at him through her tears. "Thank you, Fred. I'm proud you're my brother."

CHAPTER 17
Sammy Joe

The buckboard rattled over the cobblestones of the landing, making it sound like every board was shaking loose. The matched team of horses strained against the heavy load. Fred drove while Alroy and Zeb rode in the back to steady the blown-out boiler. The foundry was at the opposite end of the landing from the furniture factory.

"Never in all my born days did I think I'd ever see this old boiler getting fixed," Alroy said over the noise of the rattling.

"When you got two praying sisters and a praying Mama like I got, anything can happen," Fred replied.

They pulled up to the foundry, and the two men hopped out of the back. A worker came out of the foundry to help them get the boiler out and onto a cart to take inside.

"Wait here," Fred told Alroy and Zeb after the boiler was taken in. "I'll only be a minute." Papa had told Fred to take care of the business of having the boiler repaired, so he went into the offices to do that very thing.

When it was time to take the men back to the factory, Fred told them, "I want to drive past the railroad station. It's just a few blocks out of our way."

"Aye, laddie. We're in no hurry to go back," Alroy said with a smile.

Every day, sometimes twice a day, Fred went by the station to see if Sammy Joe might be there. He didn't dare hope, but he kept looking anyway. By now Sammy was probably in some far distant city, enjoying his work on the exciting railroad.

Fred clucked to the team, then turned them to go up Wood Street. He made a circle around the station and started to go back.

Suddenly Alroy said, "You're gonna look inside, aren't you?"

Fred just shook his head.

"But laddie, if I'm sittin' here with you, it means the luck o' the Irish is present."

No sooner were Alroy's words spoken than Sammy Joe came busting out that station door. "Fred! Hey there, Fred."

Fred could hardly believe his eyes.

"I tried to tell you," Alroy said, enjoying a good laugh. Elbowing Fred in the ribs, he added. "We Irish can pray as well, you know."

Climbing down from the wagon, Alroy said, "We'll walk

back and tell your papa that you've found Sammy Joe. Come on, Zeb. These two laddies need time to talk."

"Thanks, Alroy," Fred called out. "I'll be along directly."

Fred steadied the team and pulled the brake. Sammy Joe hopped up in the seat beside him.

"What a sight for sore eyes you are, my friend," Fred told him. "When did you get back into town?"

"Last night. I had to come back, Fred. My gal, she don't want me being gone no more. Even if I am working for this here good railroad. I guess I'm gonna get married."

He ducked his head a little as he added, "Sure sorry I ran out on you. I was scared that old Purlee man was gonna set slave catchers after me. He threatened to after you were gone. But I can't run forever."

"Purlee's gone, Sammy Joe. He's dead."

Sammy Joe's face turned serious. "Cholera?"

Fred nodded. "I talked to him before he died, though. He had a real change of heart."

"Truly?"

"Truly."

Sammy Joe was quiet for a moment. "God does perform great miracles, doesn't He?"

"It was that. A true miracle. Mr. Purlee thanked me—and you—for saving him the day the boiler blew. Then he said to Papa that Papa should have listened to me. Made me feel real humble."

Fred slapped the ends of the leather reins across his knee. "You know, Sammy Joe, if that had been Brother Coffin dealing with Edgar Purlee, he would have loved him. But me, I fell into hate and anger."

"Doesn't matter now. My ma always told me God gives us second chances."

"Thank goodness for that." Fred took a deep breath. "And you're getting a second chance right now. I'm taking you back to the factory! Got any gear in that station?"

"No, sir. Took it home last evening."

"Good. I showed Papa the safety plugs and helped him to see why they hadn't worked properly. It calmed his fears some. He instructed me to take the boiler to be fixed. That's where we'd just been—at the foundry." He slapped his friend on the shoulder. "It'll take a couple days to fix, then I'll need your help getting it all set up again."

Sammy Joe gave his friend a big smile. "And I'll sure give you all the help you need."

CHAPTER 18
News from California

From that day on, Papa began bringing Fred into his office at least once a week to talk over business matters. Though Papa was still a man of few words, he did tell Fred that he never wanted to die with as many regrets and as much remorse as Edgar Purlee had. The man's death had affected Papa deeply.

"God gave him time to get it all straightened out," Papa said. "But I'd rather not take that chance."

Once during their talks, Papa happened to say, "You truly are like your grandpapa Allerton, Fred. Not only was he a talker, but he was an astute and thorough businessman."

Papa couldn't have said anything that would have made Fred prouder.

Once the repaired boiler was in place and Sammy Joe and Fred had it going full steam, Fred thanked Papa for trusting him again.

Papa smiled. "Trusting you is easier now that you seem to have learned to bridle your tongue."

And it was true. Whenever Fred wanted to lash out about someone or something, he thought of Molly and how wrong he'd been about her. Now that her papa and sister were gone, she didn't come around as much anymore, and he missed her.

Julia spent all the time that Mama would allow working at the Purlees' to help with the children. One Saturday, Fred loaded up a toolbox and some toys that they had outgrown and went along with Julia. After they delivered the toys to the young Purlee children, Fred repaired the rickety front steps.

Molly sat on the porch and talked to him while he worked. It was about the most pleasant afternoon Fred could ever remember. He thought he might repair the windows for them before winter.

Papa had started coming home in the evenings—not just for supper, but for the whole evening. Papa and Fred would walk home from the factory together every evening after Sammy Joe sounded the last whistle. Mama never said much about her husband's change of habit, but Fred could see the gladness in her eyes.

There was a feeling of frost in the air as Fred and Papa walked toward the house one evening in October. The last reported case of cholera had been in September. A good hard freeze would take care of the rest, Dr. Lankford told them.

As they turned on Everett Street, they saw Julia out in the chilly evening air with no shawl, no bonnet. *Just like Julia,* Fred thought.

As soon as she saw them, she started running straight at them. In her hand she was waving a piece of paper. "From the Hendrickses!" she shouted for all the world and the neighbors to hear. "A letter from the Hendrickses!"

Fred was certain if she didn't slow down she'd run over both him and Papa. But he was thankful to have his happy sister back again. He knew she would never be the same carefree little girl that she had been—not after suffering the loss of her dear friend. But at least Julia was able to laugh again.

Over supper the Allertons read together the news from their friends, who had arrived safely in Sacramento. The letter was full of stories of hardship, peril, and suffering along the way.

Meg had already been alone with her letter from Damon. In a few months, he wrote, he would be sending money for her to come to him by ship.

Fred, his stomach full of Mama's good cooking, slathered one more slice of dark bread with the tasty *Schmierkas* and leaned back in his chair contentedly to listen as Julia read the long letter.

As he looked around at his family, he realized he'd lost the longing to run away. At what point it left, he couldn't really say. Even a job on the railroad didn't seem so enticing now. The change may have come because of a gentle and very pretty girl by the name of Purlee. But he would never admit it. And if it hadn't been for his little sister, he might never have met that pretty girl. But, of course, he wouldn't admit to that, either!

Julia glanced over the top of the letter just then and gave him her impish smile, the smile that made him know he didn't have to admit to anything.

Good News for Readers

There's more! The American Adventure continues with *Danger on the Railroad*. Charles Fisk likes to run risks with the trains on the railroad tracks outside Cincinnati. But when his sister Tina accidentally discovers that a friend's family is involved in the Underground Railroad, the two Fisks run into more trouble than either one had bargained for. When they see an escaping slave being followed by a slave catcher, Tina and Charles know they must help. But what can they do without raising the slave catcher's suspicions?

You're in for the ultimate
American Adventure!
Collect all 48 books!